Madeline's Prayer

A Novel by Marye Hefty

Endurance Publishing

Endurance Publishing
P.O. Box 6075
Olympia, WA 98507

ISBN-10: 0692280936
ISBN-13: 978-0692280935

Printed in the United States of America.

Book cover design and illustration by Christina Van Vleck

DEDICATION

To my mother who revived this book with her belief, and to all the mothers and grandmothers who raised me.

CONTENTS

Chapter 1
Rosemarie's Prayer

Rosemarie brushed her bent and twisted fingers against the wet, yellow-brown leaves that coated the metal bench, clearing just enough space for herself and the cloth grocery bag. She placed the bag on the bench and then carefully held onto the back of the bench with one hand, steadied herself and sat. A decade before this maneuver would have taken no hands and no thought. Now it required complete concentration and some luck.

Late autumn's chill stung her wet hand. Oh, how her hands ached. Repeatedly she stretched out her fingers, no longer straight but still functional, and closed them until the pain settled down. She placed her hands palms up in her lap, resting them on her raincoat. A steady stream of cars swished by on the road in front of the bench, multicolored blurs of motion spraying up a week of relentless rain. Raindrops playfully tapped down on her plastic scarf and pricked into her aching palms.

"Yes, you are playful rain, but I'm too blind and too tired to play anymore. You're wasted on me," she said. The rain fell faster and felt heavy. "Rain, rain, go away, come again another day," she recited this childhood song, sighed, and added, "You return the same every year, and I return changed. Don't you see?"

Sight. That is a problem. She pulled the "emergency" cell phone her daughter had given her from her raincoat pocket, opened the cover, and read the large numbers—2:35—from the corner of her left eye. So far, the only use for the gadget was telling the time, and it displayed this quite well.

The bus should arrive in 10 minutes, and although she looked forward to its shelter, she felt in no particular rush to reach her destination. On the other side of the ride was Claire, her daughter. Rosemarie breathed in deeply.

Claire, a daughter with all the best intentions, had managed to completely turn over nature's order, and now in less time than a rainy season, took on a new responsibility, one Rosemarie overheard her define during a phone call with a friend: "I am NOW taking care of my mother," with a strung out emphasis on "now."

"Now taking care of," said Rosemarie, turning the cell phone slowly over in her palm. "I should feel blessed," she said with tired resignation as the spray from a passing truck drowned her voice.

"Some do have it worse," she thought, returning to comfort in this comparison: "Some have it much worse." She turned the cell phone over and over in her palm, soothed by the action.

She reflected on the recent destruction and reconstruction of her life. With the efficiency of a corporate takeover, Claire hired personal organizers to downsize her mother's possessions, hired a broker to sell the house, hired estate auctioneers to sell valuable and "unnecessary" possessions to pay for the destruction, hired the movers, and hired a financial planner to manage the finances. In less than three months, the team of hired hands had managed the entire transition.

Now, returning to the city where she once

raised her daughter, Rosemarie lived in Claire's spare bedroom with her few remaining possessions, just the absolute essentials, a lifetime downsized into a guest room.

"Incredibly efficient," thought Rosemarie, but this was no surprise. Claire had always been efficient. She was organized, focused, a real professional.

Zzzzzzzzz. The cell phone vibrated in her hand, and a few seconds later she heard its faint ring muffled through the swoosh of passing cars. It was her first call since Claire had insisted she carry the phone. "Hello?"

"Grandma?" said Madeline, her granddaughter and Claire's only child.

"Hi!"

"Grandma....a few minutes late getting home....maybe 30 minutes....take care of you."

She couldn't hear every word, but she could hear enough.

"No problem, honey. I'll be waiting for you when you get home. Love you."

Rosemarie would be back in the house before her granddaughter came home from school, and no one needed to know that she had acted independently, figured out the bus schedule, escaped the house, and successfully executed an afternoon outing to the grocery store. Not that she lacked any necessities; she simply needed to get out and take care of herself, be in charge of herself, for the day.

"That poor kid," thought Rosemarie, "she has more chores than a farmer during harvest, and now she's required to watch me after school." Rosemarie reflected on her only grandchild—so full of light and promise, and so incredibly sensitive; all blessings and all curses. She is like her mother Claire had been at age 12, full of energy, interests, and compassion, and so very unlike her today.

A wind gust tore dead leaves from the old trees behind the bench, and these fell around her with the rain. Without grace, driven down in the rain, they plunged or spiraled to the ground. Rosemarie caught glimpses of their color and form—shades of yellow speckled with brown— dead by the season, removed by the weather, and scattered onto the rain-saturated earth.

For a moment, the gust cleared away the car exhaust and filled the air with the musty aroma of dead, wet leaves. This smell transported Rosemarie to a long ago memory, one she had not revisited for years. In her memory, as vivid as this exact moment, she was 12, and her father had taken her to see what he called "one of nature's great wonders." After church on their Sunday drive, he took Rosemarie and her mother to Fall Creek. When she opened the car door, she smelled the drenched leaves, musty and fresh with rain. She followed her parents down a rain-soaked dirt path blanketed in yellow and brown leaves. As they moved closer to the river, whiffs of rotting fish overwhelmed her nose and throat. She tried to breathe around it, but soon the smell engulfed her.

The memory came alive, and in her mind she watched and smelled and felt it all again. Arriving at the creek's shore, she watched as a breeze released showers of dead leaves from their branches, twirling down and landing gently on the surface of the swift water. The leaves floated atop the current, slipping between boulders and sailing over submerged smooth stones, bouncing their way around fallen logs and branches.

Breathing in small gasps to overcome the fish stench, she selected one leaf to follow on its journey, hoping it could navigate its way over and around and under all of the water's obstacles and win. As the leaf sailed gracefully atop the water

and away from her, she noticed within the water
the flashings of light and silver and red — turbu-
lence within the dark forest green water, reflecting
back the dense trees. Under the flowing surface,
the water bubbled with a struggle. Suddenly she
saw what her father had brought her to see. Under
the dance of leaves within the dark green and
clear water, fish filled every space. They completely filled the river. Facing against the strong
current, these tightly packed creatures swam
suspended in place, wiggling their forms and fins
in a struggle to remain in place. Then, one or two
would dart and flick, leaping forward to a place
ahead and up against the current.

Her father, somehow knowing she had seen,
said, "They are Pacific Salmon, and they are
returning to their home where they were born to
lay eggs, to spawn. After they do this, they die
where they were born. They are returning home to
die."

The air tasted pungent with rot. Rosemarie felt
horrified and curious and nauseous. "Why are
they struggling so hard just to die?" She could
hear the question now as clearly as she had once
asked. She couldn't remember her father's answer.

The spray from a passing truck brought her

back into the moment. She breathed in a deep and long breath. Now, she knew the answer; she lived the answer at that moment on that bench in the rain. She understood the struggle, that deeply calm, silent, invisible-except-in-flashes, dark struggle for life. She felt exhausted, absolutely immobilized against the strong and growing current of her losses.

In her youth, like the salmon, she flowed toward life and lived in its strong current. It carried her and buoyed her and energized her. But, at some season in life, maybe starting after her own parents' deaths, she began struggling with the currents of loss—strong, silent loss. And, shame, the shame of not being able to overcome the overwhelming grief and rely on a God she loved. The shame fell like rain, that late-autumn, bone-chilling rain, which swelled the currents of her losses.

At age 74, she understood how the elderly could die quietly without a final struggle, without demanding more—more time, more life—from life. She thought about her younger self, that math teacher, that force that faced struggles, that community leader, that mother, that church leader, that wife, that difference maker, that lady—

drowning now in the rising force of losses—her husband of 40 years dead, a vocation retired, friends far too many dead, mobility lost to arthritis, eyesight lost to macular degeneration, the ability to drive lost, confidence lost, value in society lost, independence lost, and even her daughter felt like a loss. Currents and currents of death and loss flowed against her.

She sat, washed and flooded in loss, feeling worn out from the burden. She had become a burden; all that remained was a burden.

Then, in a second, like the flash of a salmon within dark and deep currents, a thought burst forth with energy and brought her insight, into the rain, into autumn, into the moment. It was a thought so simple and powerful she wondered why it had not occurred to her before. She focused, carefully studying the idea. It really was a decision. It was her decision, and she could be done with loss and not be a burden. It had been a simple decision all along.

She heard the bus approaching, the un-tuned engine grinding muffled within the splash of oversized wheels. She didn't have much time.

"God, it is time," she said annunciating each word, as one announces the most important declarations. "It Is Time."

She thought about her need to speak clearly to God, for in spite of all the loss, she knew one thing: God answered prayers. Maybe God didn't answer them in the time period we wanted or in the ways we imagined, but God answered prayers. This one truth she had never lost.

She needed to be perfectly clear. "God," she clarified, knowing that once the words were spoken she wouldn't take them back. "God, I am ready to die."

Somehow the words needed a little more explanation. "You can take me now. God, forgive my selfishness. Thank you for my life and its blessings. I am eternally grateful, and now I have one last prayer that I need your help with. I am ready to die. I have had a good life, and I do not want to be a burden. I leave this in your hands. I know you will know what to do, and I thank you. Amen."

There, she had said it. She waited for the panic, for the urge to grab back her prayer, but she didn't feel it. Instead, she felt relaxed; she had given up the struggle and floated lightly in the comfort of the decision. Death wouldn't surprise her. It wouldn't arrive unwelcome. It wouldn't drown her. It would not be a loss. She would not be a burden. Hopefully, her death wouldn't be too painful or long and drawn out. She contemplated praying an addendum, asking God to make it fast and painless, but she knew God would figure out the details.

"No one will be impacted. No one will notice after a few days," she added quickly, in response to an overwhelming surge of guilt, actually a knowing, that inviting death was not an appropriate prayer.

"No one will notice," she said again, placating her guilt, as she turned and grabbed the back of the bench to stand.

"Madeline!" The word flashed in brightness, lightning illuminating all thoughts dark. A second later the bus thundered and screeched to a stop before her.

Madeline would notice.

Chapter 2
Claire's Prayer

"Damn!" Claire mouthed, pressing with exaggerated force the "end call" icon on her cell phone. She had stepped out of a meeting in the Human Services conference room to take this call from her daughter. Now standing in a hall, exposed to any number of listeners from within rows of cubicles, Claire wouldn't voice her frustration, but with a 12-year-old daughter, she had lots of experience silently mouthing it.

She had made it perfectly clear to Madeline that it was her new responsibility to be home with her grandmother on afternoons after school—perfectly clear. However, moments ago, Madeline

ambushed her with "mandatory" tryouts for a
school play on this very afternoon.

"What about your grandmother? What about
your promise?" Claire whispered.

"What, Mom?" Madeline responded,
obviously not hearing from within the voices of
other students.

Claire decided she didn't have time to argue,
to clarify, or to involve her office in any family
drama. She would deal with it later.

She took in a deep breath, a relaxation tech-
nique that a marriage counselor suggested she use
when flooded by anger. It wasn't working. She
took another. It still wasn't working.

"What will it take for Madeline to be responsible?" thought Claire, turning her cell phone over
in her hand.

She wasn't sure most of the time if she felt
raging anger at her or terrifying worry, but she
was certain of feeling completely inadequate to do
anything to help. Whatever she felt, the result was
the same: Claire hated herself as a mother for not
being able to handle her daughter with the profes-
sionalism with which she could handle her job.
And, although she told herself that next time she
would handle the situation better, she almost

always responded to her daughter in the same two ways: 1) with explosive anger, or 2) with checked anger accompanied by long lectures about how hard the world had become and how her daughter was proving to be woefully inept at navigating through it. But, as Claire knew and her daughter demonstrated, the anger and the lectures made Madeline withdraw and Claire feel more inadequate as a mother.

Sometimes during her most frustrating moments, when her feelings from interacting with Madeline ranged the minuscule distance from furious to failing, she marveled at how much she had wanted this daughter, her only baby, and how much emotion, work, and money she and John had put into conceiving her. Yes, 12 years ago, Claire felt an instant and overwhelming bond with Madeline the first time she held her. In fact, when Madeline was a baby, Claire often felt surprised by these floods of joy. This was her baby. Her girl. Her wonderful, special girl. Standing in the office hallway now, she simply felt mad enough to yell or throw something or a combination of the two.

"Calm down," she told herself, after realizing that her heart was beating into her throat. "Get control," she told herself without uttering a word.

She looked out over the maze of cubicles, leaned against the outside of the conference room wall and breathed, consciously inhaling a few deep breaths and exhaling slowly. She knew she must calm down before returning to the meeting.

"How can I make this child get it?" Claire thought.

A word flashed in her thoughts: "Pray." She frowned, turned over the cell phone, and looked at the time on its display. She didn't have time to pray. Actually, she didn't have time right now to worry about her daughter, and this really got her heart pounding again.

Unlike her mother, or maybe as a result of her mother, Claire saw no use in prayer, absolutely no use at all. Wasted time—and she didn't have time to waste. She had already wasted way, way too much time today—all billable hours wasted. From what she had witnessed watching her mother Rosemarie pray, through all the years and mountains of prayers, it was all superstition; no one was listening—just wasted words uttered by simple-minded people. However, to compartmentalize this anger and move on to productive time, she needed to do something, and prayer seemed like a way to hand off the problem to someone else, even if that someone else didn't exist. Therefore, with an effort like throwing a penny into some cheap wishing well, she began whispering an angry wish, the closest she could come to a prayer.

"God," she barely uttered the word when the door to the conference room opened. Immediately, she stood tall, pushed back her shoulders, felt energy, and put on her well-practiced "relaxed and in control" look.

"Is everything okay?" said Vicki, her boss, approaching. At five foot nine without heels, Vicki towered over most other women and stood two inches taller than Claire; today she towered in black stilettos, balancing her form in a Nordstrom/Macy's blend black business skirt suit, and jet black bobbed hair, all packaged perfectly for the board meeting. Claire stood her ground in similar business fashion, a sleek black suit, painstakingly packaged from the Macy's sale racks. She accessorized her "look" with straight shoulder-length brown hair and makeup simply for color, all professional but natural, so as to appear more open and less cold to clients.

"Yes, just fine." Claire adjusted her suit jacket and focused on her smile, natural and relaxed. "My daughter checks in when her plans change."

"That's good," said Vicki without pause, although Claire was sure Vicki hadn't registered a word before continuing: "You've put together a winning draft in there, and I think we have a winner if we can wrap up this meeting, and if you can get the changes made by the deadline. The deadline is do-able, right?"

Claire recognized the command. It was not a question. It was a demand, an essential act for future employment. The pace of work had become unrelenting with one essential deadline overlapping the previous deadline and the next. It didn't matter that seven of her last ten grants had been successfully funded. What mattered today was that she meet THIS deadline to get THIS grant funded.

Success once meant a respite—an ebb tide. At one time she remembered viscerally, the year had tides with moments of extreme effort, the success, and then calm, each coming as a wave. Not now. Each day brought a new wave, a storm surge of new tasks and ever-growing not-yet-accomplished task lists. Limited budgets no longer allowed for the ebb time after the success.

Claire let the command hang between them for a few seconds.

"Claire?" Vicki asked.

"We'll meet the deadline," Claire said looking up and meeting Vicki's eyes. Claire didn't blink until Vicki nodded and looked down.

"I'll be back to finish the meeting in a minute," Claire said nonchalantly, stepping around her boss and walking down the hall into the bath-room. Scanning the bathroom stalls, she quickly assessed she was alone.

"Breathe, breathe," she whispered while taking deep breaths and placing both hands on the cold, marble sink counter. She looked into the mirror.

"God, I look exhausted," she thought frown-ing at the puffiness under her eyes. Relaxing into her breathing, she felt a soul-aching exhaustion, always the result in these rare moments of stillness.

"Okay focus," she demanded to the reflection in the mirror. She needed to focus on the task in front of her, put her frustration with Madeline aside for now, check it off, and get back to work. She had to compartmentalize and return to the task of keeping her job.

"Okay, my prayer," she said, announcing to the mirror the first step in her plan to get back into the conference room. With urgency, she spoke her prayer, which sounded powerful echoing against the marble and into the vacant stalls.

"God, teach my daughter to be responsible. This is a tough world and getting tougher each day, and she needs to learn responsibility if she is going to be successful. Yes, teach my daughter to be responsible."

There, it was done, compartmentalized until after work. She was in control. To meet the deadline, she would need to take control and stop the board members from commenting on minutia. She ran her fingers through her hair, brushing it away from her face. It didn't need coloring yet, although a few silver strands were visible at the part. Her eye shadow looked smooth and natural, not too much and not too little, just enough to highlight her green eyes.

Breathing in deeply and consciously several times more, she focused on the moment: she needed to walk back into the meeting and shut it down so that she could incorporate relevant comments and meet tomorrow's deadline. She smiled mechanically into the mirror to double check. There was nothing between her teeth.

Chapter 3
Madeline's Prayer

As Mr. Edwards, the substitute English teacher, painstakingly reviewed line by line the details of proper outlining, like an analysis of some famous poem, Madeline actually focused on her own poem, silently sounding out each word.

"What kind of poet would you be, in this year, Emily?..."

She listened silently to the rolls and waves of the words. It almost felt right, almost.

By writing poetry in long hand at home in her journal, and then reciting it silently in class to refine it, Madeline could handle the recent hours of in-class test preparation and skill set reviews.

Without her poems, each minute she spent trying to sit still and listen to test reviews or to subjects she somehow already knew stretched out longer, thinner, and slower until the struggle to stay awake in an elongated second (when added to 59 other seconds) just hurt. Each minute physically hurt.

Mr. Edwards had asked a question. She didn't hear the question, but he had stopped talking, moved away from the outline projected onto a screen from his computer, and entreated, hands out and palms up, to the class for answers. Madeline, who sat in the middle of the classroom, looked left and then right at the other seventh graders, and wished in the anxious silence that she had heard the question.

Finally, the voice of a boy behind her said, "If you are going to have a letter A, you need a letter B; otherwise, it's an example."

"What do you mean 'it's an example'?" Mr. Edwards asked, obviously pleased with the discussion.

Madeline turned to watch Robert, the boy sitting behind her, which gave her an excuse to pan the room. In turning her torso, she pretended to have eyes like a panoramic camera, documenting the full depth and breadth of the room, just like a director might study a location for a movie. "No," she said to herself, in the imaginary voice a movie director might use, "none of these displays will do," referring to the walls organized and brightened by war timelines, posters of famous generals, the famous casualty graph from the Russian Revolution, and country flags. "This is 'outline class' men; not a death march!"

She smiled at Robert. He looked right over her. She turned back to face Mr. Edwards.

Mr. Edwards, satisfied with the answer Robert had given, returned to his example outline. Madeline returned to thinking about her poem.

She started it weeks ago after a class in which her regular English teacher, Mrs. Colby, discussed the life of Emily Dickinson. Madeline found it fascinating that someone born in such a different time in such different circumstances could write about feelings so much like hers. As Mr. Edwards stopped for responses to another question, she laid her hands palms down on the desk, and applied pressure to her left thumb. "Okay," she thought, "Ways by each finger I am like Emily…"

Left thumb—poets.

Left index –chestnut brown hair; warm, brown

eyes; bold, brown eyebrows; very plain; a little pale—all one index finger of physical features.

Left middle—isolated.

Left ring—aware.

Left pinky—unsure.

Right thumb—different.

Right index—lonely sometimes.

Right middle—invisible today.

Right ring—did Emily attend a middle school?

Right pinky... .

Madeline stumbled and paused on the right pinky, accepting that maybe sharing a hair color, feeling lonely, being isolated, and liking to write poems didn't exactly result in a DNA match.

The right pinky—UNCONVENTIONAL.

The word appeared in her mind, and she straightened her back thinking that she too shared this trait with this dead poet she admired. Yes, unconventional, a great five-syllable word.

Turning over her hand, she moved her right pinky, like mini-calisthenics, up down, up down.

"No," she thought, "no matter how many pinky exercises I do, I am not unconventional. Emily ignored conventions of the time, and Madeline wished she could. No, instead, she worked to blend in and aspired to appear normal, and it was hard to appear normal when all her physical parts just didn't seem to fit well together, like a poster child for the "not exactly normal."

Madeline hated junior high, or more precisely (she liked the word "precisely"), she hated herself for not fitting in like everyone around her seemed to be doing perfectly well. Unfortunately, she felt one step closer to strange than to normal. Since arriving at 7th grade and this new school, she worked hard to fit in, but she didn't feel "in" at all. Her only real friends were friends from grade school, and all of them were in different home rooms and classes.

She hoped being involved in the school play might help. Chelsea, a grade-school friend, asked her to try out, and although a little terrifying, it offered some hope of future belonging. She wished she could be like all the other kids, but she felt more like Emily Dickinson.

"Yes, my best friend is a dead poet," thought Madeline, smiling at this, an unusual thought. "I do have unconventional thoughts."

Mr. Edwards had moved behind her, and was asking someone another question. To concentrate on her poem and block every other thought out,

she placed her elbows on the desk, looked down,
cupping her hands around her face. Then, in a
voice to herself, she recited her new poem,
listening to the fit and fall and pause of each
syllable and sound.

What kind of poet would you be
In this year
Emily?

Would you grasp this time of choices
With a modern tool?
Perhaps an editor
Maybe a journalist
Possibly a playwright
Limited only by possibilities
Think of all the probabilities.

In time, would such things remain?
With a change of scenery
Could the poet remain?
Reflecting,
Where the glare is bright.

Emily,
Do we create our time…

Or does time create us?
What kind of poet would you be?
In this year….
Emily.

The bell rang. Madeline flinched, instinctively preparing to flee. She dreaded what would happen next, even more than she dreaded sitting in class pretending to be interested.

A cacophony of voices filled the classroom and echoed out into the silent hall. She was strategically seated to reach the hall with five long and quick steps from her chair. Without thought, completely by survival instinct, Madeline bolted for the door. If she hurried, she could make it to her locker and to the gym for play practice before most of the students even left their classrooms, but she needed to think through her route. She focused.

"Wait!" Mr. Edwards yelled. Madeline stopped, the escape advantage lost, stolen by his command.

"Class, remember," he spoke loudly and way, way too slowly, "We have a test on Friday."

That was all it took. With Mr. Edwards stopping her to state the obvious, now the advantage was gone. She dropped her head and stepped out the door. Students flowed out from rows of classroom doors into the long hallway. They blocked all direct paths to the lockers.

Madeline walked with purpose. She focused on the feet in front of her, jostling and maneuvering through the crowds, and glancing up just quickly enough to define a path. She moved along the wall, but at the next classroom, three students talking with a teacher blocked the wall route. Darting into a center clearing, she brushed by the obstruction of two 8th-grade boys walking slowly. Her heart beat into her ears. She could actually feel her ears throbbing. "Interesting," she thought, and in the disruption of this thought, she lost focus and ran into someone. At impact, with her head down, she noticed two very large Nike tennis shoes—like probably size 13. They looked like basketball shoes. The body she hit did not move, and she bounced back with the impact and into another student.

"Hey!" The boy behind her yelled pushing her forward. She swayed with the shove inches from the chest of the large kid with Nike shoes. Slowly she followed the shoes to the jeans to the letterman's jacket—football not basketball—to his face, ready to say, "I'm sorry," but before she could form the words, a girl standing next to him shouted in surliness, "Hey, what ARE you doing?'

Before Madeline could answer, the football letterman answered, "It's okay, she didn't mean it."

"What do you mean, she didn't mean it?" said the girl, turning to look up into his face.

"I'm sorry," said Madeline, but neither heard.

"I said she didn't mean it," he repeated defensively.

Madeline carefully stepped around them, repeating, "I'm sorry," but neither noticed.

Ahead of her, two stoner girls walked toward her in a side-by-side wall immersed in conversation. Instinctively, she thought to jog to the right, but not after the last collision. Stopping, positioned with her hands blocking her chest, she warned, "Excuse me." They parted and moved past her. Madeline's ears still throbbed, and she turned a corner to the school's center and the hive of lockers, dozens and dozens of lockers in rows.

Seeing her locker, she moved toward it, focused and physically feeling the vibration from countless conversations sliced by the metal opening and shutting of the steel locker doors. Four girls deep in lively discussion completely blocked access to her locker. Instantly and silently, like a trained athlete, she sized up the situation: "They are four 8th graders—all popular. One's from English class; she'll let me in, but she's not the block; the others will be. They are loud. They are laughing. They are popular." Each "they are" thought beat loudly within her pounding heart. "They are turning. They are now focusing away. They are focusing on the boys lined up across from them. Now!" Her heart skipped with her own thoughts, "Move, an opening, now!"

Madeline miscalculated the risk and timing. At exactly the moment she reached the opening to her locker, the four girls shifted and blocked it. Then, she heard the boys arrive behind her. And there, like a trapped rabbit, she stood facing the four girls who all at once, like a wild pack, took their focus off their prizes standing directly behind Madeline and now looked confused by the "thing" in front of them.

"Excuse me," Madeline said, but no one moved, obviously not from any group defiance but from complete shock at her gall. Awkwardly, she reached out between the two girls directly in front of her locker. They parted, and although she didn't make eye contact, she could feel their glares. For the eternity it took to open the locker, she felt only her heart beating in her ears.

"Focus, focus, focus," she told herself while steadying her shaking hand to open the locker. Thankfully, it opened on her first try. She transferred out her jacket. Shutting the locker, she turned to face the gauntlet of 8th graders that had now formed a half circle around her.

No one spoke. She looked up at four girls and four boys.

"Hi, sorry," said Madeline, walking out to clear a path through the circle. Two boys moved, and as she slid through, one of the girls asked, "Are you retarded?" without meanness and in a tone of real wonder.

No one laughed. Madeline stopped outside the circle. A few others had noticed the exchange from their lockers, and she could feel them watching her carefully like one might watch a wounded rabbit.

She tried to breathe, deep breaths like she had seen her mother do, but this wasn't working. Feeling dizzy, she looked for an open and empty classroom. She saw an open door and focused all energy on making it inside. No one was in the room. From the world maps on the walls, she knew it was a social studies homeroom. She closed the door and fell into a seat and lay her head on the desk. Her ears pounded. The dizziness continued. She wheezed in deep breaths.

Her entire body ached, and she desperately wanted to cry, but the first play practice was scheduled to start soon, and if she cried, her eyes would be bloodshot and her face might blotch red, and she couldn't have anyone notice how alone and scared and out of place she really felt. Continuing to focus on breathing, she began to feel some control, and as the anxiety subsided, to feel profoundly sad. Sitting up and slouching back, she crossed her arms and felt all the sorrow sweep over the moment. For five minutes, she sat and felt her chest rise and fall, breathing in and out overwhelming pain.

"God," she said slowly and carefully to the worlds on the walls, "I don't think I'm going to make it." There was no plea in her voice, simply honest resignation with great sadness. It seemed okay to tell God this. Obviously, no one could understand. She couldn't understand. A year ago she had loved school within her 6th grade class. She loved Mrs. Robinson and felt accepted and safe with her 28 classmates and three good friends. Now, two months into her new school, where 7th graders from seven districts merged, she had multiple classes with multiple teachers in a school with hundreds and hundreds of students, and none of them friends from grade school and none of them friends from junior high. She had made no new friends. None.

"Pray." The thought popped in her mind but in her grandmother's voice.

"Grandma!" She remembered the obligation to watch her after school. The school had a "no cell phone use" policy, but feeling inside her jacket pocket for the phone, she decided in a minute to turn on her phone and call her mother, telling her that she would be late watching Grandma, but first she needed to say her prayer.

Madeline really loved her grandmother, who believed in her and in prayer. "At all times and all places and all circumstances"—it was a line Grandma said sometimes after she told Madeline she loved her or when she announced that she was praying for her.

Madeline was glad to have her staying now in their home. She smiled hearing her grandma's favorite saying: "Always remember, God loves you and answers your prayers. You are never alone with God."

"Grandma, what should I pray?" Her heart no longer beat into her ears, and she listened to the question echo into the emptiness of the room. She thought about the possibilities and all the prayers that God must answer. Her needs seemed minuscule compared to the needs of others. Looking at the world maps wallpapering the room, she imagined God overwhelmed with prayers, with a deafening noise of really serious prayers. Noting different locations on the world map, she imagined the constant prayers God must hear—prayers for rain from people in Australia, prayers for peace in the Gaza strip and Middle East, prayers for better pay in the factories in China, prayers for jobs in America, a trillion times a trillion prayers.

"I wonder what all those prayers sound like? The thought distracted until sometime later she came back to the moment with the thought, "If God hears all prayers, what will be my prayer?"

No answer came, but surprisingly, the question soothed. It was such an enormous question with millions of possible answers. It was an important question. She felt okay, a little raw in her skin, sensitive in space, but okay.

The noise in the hallway outside had faded to a few slamming lockers, a few shouts, and a few laughs. It was safe; she could call her mother and go to play tryouts now.

"What will be my prayer?" she asked aloud into the empty room and felt comforted by the question, by the silence, and by the unlimited possibilities.

Chapter 4
Madeline's Secret

At play tryouts, Madeline volunteered and was selected as a member of the lighting crew, happy to start her experience with drama from behind the stage. More important, she saw Chelsea, her friend from grade school, and although they didn't have the opportunity to say more than a few words, the words they did exchange replaced the dark residue from her afterschool debacle.

"Maddie!" Chelsea smiled and raced over as soon as Madeline entered the auditorium. And after an awkward second standing a foot apart, Chelsea filled the silence with seven magical words, "Will you eat lunch with me tomorrow?"

"Yes," she said.

"Look over here all of you and listen up," said the drama coach.

Madeline turned to face him, relieved that Chelsea would not notice she was about to cry.

By the time Madeline began the half-mile walk home, the rain had stopped, although everything, from the sidewalk to the air, was soaked. Walking toward the one major intersection between school and home, she saw the back of a man who was leaning against the signal pole blocking the walk button. She thought about crossing the street to avoid him, but decided he would leave when the light turned green again. The light turned green; he didn't move, and now she stood less than 10 feet behind him on the sidewalk. It would look silly to cross the street to avoid him. Besides, it was almost 5:00 p.m., and enough light from dusk and the street lights illuminated the man, and the constant stream of cars speeding by at 10 miles over the 25-mile limit still traveled slow enough for the drivers to notice him. "I'm safe," she told herself.

Arriving close but a step behind and an arm's distance away, she sized him up in the instant as he turned to face her. About her father's height—a tall six-footer and thin, he was clean-shaven with short dark hair, like her father's military cut. The few acne pocks in his cheeks were old and scarred, not full and festering like the faces of some boys her age. College-aged she guessed. From the side, he appeared ordinary, normal, not like some scary stranger. He wore jeans and a light brown jacket over a tan T-shirt. A camouflage-designed backpack and a guitar case covered in torn and slapped-on destination stickers rested on the wet pavement next to him. He wore black military-issue shoes, worn but polished. He held a homemade cardboard sign, which he extended toward traffic and now toward her: "Vet to Seattle."

"You goin' to Seattle?" he asked loudly, turning toward her and grinning at his own humor.

"No," said Madeline, looking down quickly and thinking that maybe not making eye contact was the second best thing to not talking to strangers; it was rude not to reply.

"I'm headin' home; need to see....," he said, with some words muffled in the splash of the passing cars.

"Name's Frank. Yours?"

Madeline wished the signal light would turn green, but his body blocked the button, and no cars were coming from the road behind her to trigger the sensors. She watched the steady stream of cars passing in the road in front of them. She could feel him looking down at her and she considered not answering, but he was only being kind, something too many kids in junior high hadn't learned to do. He had a kind voice like her father.

"Madeline," she said.

"And, ya go to that junior high up the hill?"

"Yeah."

"Tell me," he paused. What group you in?"

"Excuse me?"

"You know. Do you fit in—'LOVE junior high' or 'HATE junior high?' What group?" he said emphasizing the contrasts. He looked out at the cars and held his sign a little more out into the street.

"I guess, hate it," she said, surprised that she answered. She expected another question, but he focused on the passing cars, and she wondered, "Is there really an entire group that hates junior high? A group more than one?"

He looked over at her again, and put his sign

to his side, as if he might say something important. Instead, he stood up from the pole, moved aside, and used his sign in an exaggeratedly respectful gesture that she should push the button and walk across.

She waited, avoiding eye contact by staring at the walk button. He waited. He finally spoke.

"Ya know, it takes a lifetime sometimes to recover from junior high, an entire damn life."

She didn't move. He didn't move. She looked up into his face. He looked sad, but not just sad in general, but sad for her. She instinctively felt the difference. Neither moved for a long 30 seconds. He watched her. Then, turning away and extending his sign out toward the road again, he changed to a joking tone, and said, "If you keep standin' here with me, my odds of hitchin' a ride are astronomically and mathematically higher. Yep, with a pretty girl like you standing here next to me, it's my lucky day!"

"Pretty?" she thought. She looked out watching the cars pass.

"But," he said, laughing at his own joke, "don't stand too close because my chances of getting arrested go up astronomically and mathematically too." And he laughed.

Madeline knew better than to laugh, but she liked his humor; it reminded her of her father's. She missed her father. She really, really missed him.

"You could be my daughter, I guess. Same age I think," said Frank, bringing her back to the moment. He smiled, a smile she knew was meant for her, but he directed it into the windshields of the passing cars. He waved his sign in a slow, exaggerated wave. The steady stream of cars continued to drive by.

"Yep, it's a big help to have you standing here with me," he said.

After several minutes standing together in silence, Madeline heard a car drive up from the road behind her and triggered the sensors. The crosswalk sign turned green.

"Have a nice day, Madeline," he smiled directly, deeply, and kindly, extending his sign out into the crosswalk like an invitation to walk on a fancy red carpet.

"I can stay 10 more minutes," she said softly.

"Thanks," he replied, standing tall and moving closer to her, making it appear clearly that they were together. She imagined what it would be like hitchhiking with him to Seattle.

"Wow," he exclaimed, "it worked—here's my ride!"

Madeline looked up at him and smiled broadly. She had helped someone today. This felt good to make a difference for someone else. Then, she looked out and saw the white sedan and felt nauseous.

"Madeline," he said while reaching into his jacket pocket, "Here take this as a reward for your work here," and he held out his hand quickly. She automatically moved her hand under his, and felt a business card. He moved his hand away, and she stood frozen with fear.

"Now," he requested, "Put it in your pocket. You might use it one day."

She did as he asked, and didn't have time to explain. She knew she was in trouble, very big trouble.

The car window rolled down. "Young lady!" Claire yelled from inside the car, "Get in this car this minute!"

Mortified by her mother's outburst, Madeline rushed to get into the car, hoping to leave the moment and shame.

And YOU!" she pointed a finger at Frank and shouted with a guttural rage, "YOU. Yes YOU!

Back away! Back away from this car and my daughter before I call the police! Back away NOW!"

Chapter 5
Claire's Problem

"Put on your seatbelt!"

As Claire drove away from the curb, she pointed and glared at the man who had been standing with her daughter, ensuring that he had received her clearest of messages about what wrath messing with her daughter would unleash. She shivered from the outstretched finger to the deepest reaches of her soul when he responded with a shrugged shoulder and exaggerated, sly smile.

Grasping both hands around the steering wheel, she could feel her fingernails digging into her palms. She suppressed a scream. How could her daughter be so foolish, so absolutely stupid, and so incredibly irresponsible!

"Madeline," she yelled with physical force. "What the hell are you thinking?! Do you know that man?! I saw the way he looked at you! I saw you talking to him! Have you lost your mind?! What have your father and I told you about talking to strangers?! Are you hearing me, young lady!? You're in SUCH trouble! Trouble like you've never known!"

If Madeline had an answer, Claire didn't give her the breath's time to answer.

"Jesus, Mary, and Joseph, child, what am I supposed to do with you?!" yelled Claire, banging the steering wheel. "What have your father and I taught you?! Has any of this sunk into your head?!"

Madeline said nothing, and Claire felt relieved. She didn't want to hear a good excuse or even one peep of a little excuse until she could figure out how to handle this situation, and right now she knew she was not in control. Not at all. She needed a moment to process all of this. She needed to get out of the car and away from her daughter before she slapped her and slapped her hard.

Driving past the turnoff to home, Claire focused on breathing—breathe in and breathe out—and said nothing. She needed a place to contain her daughter while she gained control of her emotions. Madeline sat silently. "At least my child is smart enough not to speak right now," thought Claire.

Ten long, silent, and stress-filled minutes later, Claire steered the car into the suburb's super store. Avoiding the usual five-minute search for parking close to the entrance, she parked in the first open space.

"Young lady, we will talk when we get home," she said in a measured and controlled cadence. "Right now, I need to get some things for dinner, and I want you to sit in this car and think about what you've done." She opened the door, stepped out, and slammed it behind her.

Walking briskly, she had at least 15 parked cars to walk by before reaching the entrance. Usually, she watched carefully for elderly drivers backing out or distracted teenagers using cell phones racing for the nearest spot, but tonight she felt like daring someone to just try and hit her.

"What am I going to do with this child?" she fumed, not even slowing when a car tried to inch out into her path and stopped abruptly to avoid hitting her. At one point, she was headed for a collision with a long line of carts herded by a reflective-vested employee who had them rolling at an angle ready to cut directly in front of her. He looked at her to signal his intention, and she glared, "Don't you dare!" He stopped, pulling back the carts' momentum, and she passed without a word.

Once inside, an elderly man wearing the store's trademark vest said, "Good evening, miss." She glared straight through him not hiding her anger as she grabbed a cart from the chute. She didn't have the time or the patience to fake polite-ness. She had emotions to process before returning to the car.

With the cart as her shield, she stepped onto the shiny vinyl floors in the wide aisles and moved with starts, rolls, turns, and stops among dozens of other shopping carts, all operated by completely forgettable people.

"Okay, what do I do?" she thought and walked. She pulled out her cell phone and pushed speed dial for her husband. She checked her watch. He didn't answer.

"John," she said after the prompting to leave a

message, "YOUR daughter is in trouble, and I need your support with this. She completely blew off taking care of Mother this afternoon, and I found her with some retro-hippy degenerate hitchhiking to Seattle. Who knows his history! I am not kidding. I am not kidding at all! John, call me back as soon as you get this message."

Claire felt dizzy. She needed to find a place to process. She could go to the food court, but this would be too crowded and the smell of greasy, cheap food too annoying. She needed to sit alone, and soon.

Placing her phone in her jacket pocket, she quickly turned her cart toward the center of the store. She moved through rows and rows of shoulder-height steel racks of women's clothing. She passed tall modular walls with hanging clothes—women's, men's, and accessories. She found the lingerie section, grabbed a bra as she passed a display, left the cart, and showed the bra to the woman checking customers into the fitting rooms.

"I want to try this on in the room farthest in the back," said Claire, noticing that she had picked up a size 44-D, and her actual size was a 36-B. The young woman looked at her, looked at the bra, looked at her chest, and looked back at her. Claire glared.

"Okay," said the girl, shaking her head while grabbing a plastic room tag.

The girl led her to the back dressing room, unlocked, and opened the door before stepping aside and handing over the bra. Claire mumbled "thank you" and closed the door.

She threw the bra on the bench, sat next to it, turned, leaned against the portable wall, pulled up her feet, and crouched into a ball on the bench.

For the first time since turning off the alarm at 6:30 a.m., she sat still. Her chest moved up and down with heavy breaths. She wanted to cry, but she couldn't cry; it would run her makeup and redden her eyes and blotch her cheeks, and take way too much time. It wasn't worth the time or effort.

"What do I do with this kid?" she whispered. "She just doesn't get it, and I don't have time for this right now." Remaining balled up, Claire placed her elbows on her knees and rested her chin in her palms, latticing her fingers over her face.

"I wish her father were here," she thought. What a whirlwind and a herculean struggle the last two years had been. It all happened so fast and so unexpectedly. One day John was working, like all other work days for eight years, as a profitable store manager for Kitchen One, the regional cooking specialty store; then, the next day, literally overnight, the corporation declared bankruptcy, and during a month-long restructuring, shut down his store. For less pay and fewer benefits, corporate offered him a job in another state. He had one week to give his answer.

That was two years ago. She and John had used up every extra hour of that week analyzing every option and dreaming every scheme. At the end of the week, John told corporate no. Had it been the right decision? Claire didn't know. That one decision, like dominoes falling, fell into the next, until all the decisions ran together and raced right up to this cascading moment. John was back in school three states away spending every cent of their life savings to earn a two-year degree as a radiologic technician, the person responsible for taking x-rays at a hospital. "Seven more months, just seven more months," she repeated.

The sanctuary of the dressing room soothed her. She felt calmer, still mad as hell at Madeline, but nowhere near hitting-her mad. She focused on breathing, deep and long breaths, and concentrated on the strategy for making it through each day lately—do what has to be done and ignore the static—ignore the feelings. Just get through the day. Keep the job. Keep the income. Keep on track.

She mentally ran through the "to do" list for the night:

- Purchase a bagged salad for the bagged chicken stir fry in the freezer.
- Figure out an appropriate punishment for Madeline.
- Figure out what is wrong with Madeline.
- Pick up mother's prescription and confirm the date of her doctor's appointment.
- Make dinner and plan tomorrow's dinner.
- Finish incorporating comments into the proposal.
- Check the mail.
- Pay the credit card bills.
- Talk to John.
- Get clothes ready for work tomorrow.
- Ensure that Madeline has finished her homework.
- Figure out who will watch her mother on afternoons if Madeline has play practice.

- And, after everyone has gone to bed, if it is still not done, get back to the proposal and finish incorporating comments.

The list was do-able with planning and time management. Stretching out her legs along the bench, careful not to lean too hard against the modular wall, she opened the notepad function in the cell phone and composed the list, reorganizing and grouping related tasks. Here she could get the salad and mother's prescription. After a few minutes, Claire only had three "to do's" on her list that still needed a plan:

- Figure out an appropriate punishment for Madeline.
- Figure out what is wrong with Madeline.
- Figure out who will watch her mother on afternoons if Madeline has play practice.

Claire studied the items, concentrating on solutions.

"Miss, are you okay?" said the clerk, knocking on the fitting room door.

Claire startled up straight, and the wall wobbled.

"Oh, I'm fine. I'll be out in one minute. The bra doesn't fit."

"Really?" replied the girl with an obvious tone

of sarcasm.

"I'll be right out."

"Well," said the clerk, "I'm going on break, so if you need help, you can ask Crystal in women's fashions. She will help you."

"Thank you," said Claire, glad for the respite in the shift switch. She decided to tackle the toughest of the three problems first, a skill she learned in a business management class: "Figure out what is wrong with Madeline."

In a spark of insight, at the deepest place of Claire's soul, she knew what was wrong. The recognition flashed. Soul to soul, mothers know their children. But, this was a place she had no time to visit—on this evening with all that she had to do—get the groceries, make dinner, finish the proposal, balance the checkbook, care for her mother—she could not meet her daughter at this place. Frankly, she simply had to get through this day and put food on the table and ensure that the food and shelter would be there tomorrow. Someone had to help her daughter, but on this day it would not be Claire; she had enough real problems of her own.

Claire scrolled through the list of contacts in her phone until she settled on the number of the marriage counselor she and John had seen four years ago when they could afford a marriage counselor. He had helped them understand and communicate between their differences. She pushed send, and waited for the answering machine.

"Dr. Tim Hancock's office," said the secretary, a voice she recognized.

"Sorry, I thought I'd get an answering machine."

"Yes, we changed our hours. We now start at 10:00 a.m. with the last appointment at 7:00 p.m."

"This is Claire. Dr. Hancock saw me and my husband for six months about four years ago and helped us."

"Yes, hi Claire. I remember you both. How are you?"

"Well, I'm fine. However, my daughter, who is in 7th grade this year is not doing well, and I would like her to see Dr. Hancock."

"In general, what is the problem?"

Claire knew that the secretary was assessing if and how quickly Dr. Hancock would be able to see Madeline; therefore, Claire had to carefully choose her words to not exaggerate the situation but to convey a dire urgency for treatment. She needed an appointment soon.

"I believe she may be depressed. She is not acting responsibly, and she is not listening to me. I am worried about her safety," said Claire while emphasizing with drawn out syllables and a deeper tone the words "I am worried about her."

After a pause, the familiar voice said, "Dr. Hancock had a cancellation on Thursday at 4:00. Can you bring her in then?"

"Yes, thank you."

"What is your daughter's name?"

"Madeline."

"Okay, we will see Madeline on Thursday at 4:00."

Claire pushed "end call," returned to the to-do list, and clicked a checkmark symbol next to "figure out what is wrong with Madeline." Only two items remained:

- Figure out an appropriate punishment for Madeline.
- Figure out who will watch her mother on afternoons if Madeline has play practice.

She looked at the items. Written out, it was obvious: one clearly solved the other. She thought through the logic. "Madeline's punishment will be that she cannot try out for play practice; she cannot be in this play or any play until she can act responsibly. Yes, she will be upset and yes, on the surface this seems cruel, but the real cruelty is ignoring her bad judgment, her inability to follow simple rules, and her lack of responsibility in order to placate her feelings.

"Yes," Claire smiled at the simplicity of it all. "She will need to successfully watch her grandmother until I can find the time to transfer Mom to a nursing home, which could be as long as two months because I don't have time to find a satisfactory place and fill out all the financial paperwork until this proposal process at work is complete."

Claire knew the importance of setting clear and specific goals that were reachable. She liked the sound of all this. "If at the end of two months," she reasoned, continuing to think through the details while tapping a finger quickly on the dressing room bench, "if she shows me she can act responsibly by showing up at a defined time and staying with her grandmother after school every day for two months, then she can try out for the spring play or any after school activity, and this will give me time to find long-term nursing care for Mother."

Claire relaxed. It felt like win, win, win all the way around. She clicked checkmarks in front of these items.

"Are ya in there?" said a voice outside the fitting-room door.

"Yes, just one second," said Claire. She opened the door, looked up, and flinched back startled, having instantly sized up the situation. She faced a woman her own age and height. Within the trademark vest, the woman was too thin and wore jeans aged by hard work and not for style. The woman's shoulders stooped forward greeting everyone with her broken spirit. Her frizzed hair had highlights of grey strands and yellow starts from several layers of botched home colorings. Excessive sun and smoking produced wrinkles too deep and too long to cover. Claire could tell she had been born beautiful and maybe kept this promise in youth, but now all of these features worked together through the woman's coffee-stained, crooked teeth to scream silently and with physical force at Claire: "I am poor!"

Claire straightened up and feigned a smile. The woman stared at her, understanding the silent exchange, and took the bra that Claire held out toward her as one might hold food for a wild and possibly rabid animal. Then, Claire brushed by her, turned, and rushed away.

After buying a bagged salad, she raced from the store, feeling a new resolve in her role to raise her daughter responsibly to be prepared for the challenges of today's world. Her daughter would not grow up to be poor! Period. She would be responsible.

Chapter 6
Rosemarie's Problem

Each morning Rosemarie awoke at 5:30, an internal clock set through years of habit. During the first two days staying with her daughter, she had brushed her teeth, sponge bathed, dressed, and by 6:00 waited eagerly at the kitchen table for interactions with her daughter and granddaughter.

On both mornings, she heard two alarms go off at 6:30. She sat and listened to Claire hurrying—opening drawers, slamming doors, sliding open the shower curtain, turning on the water, closing the shower curtain, turning on the shower, turning off the shower, switching on the blow dryer, yelling at Madeline to get up and get going—all in a tremendous fury as if making up for an overslept alarm.

"Come on, Madeline! It's time to get up. Now!" said Claire at the same time in the same sequence of events on both days.

On both days, at 7:30, like clockwork, Claire rushed into the kitchen and stopped. The cessation of momentum filled the space. After seconds in silence, Claire quickly said the exact same words in exactly the same tone, "Mom. Sorry I don't have time right now. Help yourself to anything." Then, as if remembering her routine, she yelled back to the bedrooms, "Madeline, you have 5 minutes to eat something. Get in here now!" Then, within the storm by which she entered the room, she exited.

It happened the same way on both of her first days in Claire's house. It hurt the first day. It even hurt the second day. It didn't need to hurt a third or a fourth day, or ever again. After Claire and Madeline had left the house on that second day, she sat at the kitchen table bemused that the strong feelings from rejection return in old age as familiar and surprisingly stinging as they had been in adolescence. Despite a lifetime of distance between adolescence and old age, the rejection stung in its new form just the same.

So on this day, Rosemarie awoke at 5:30, brushed her teeth, sponge bathed, dressed, and sat in the chair next to the bed to read. She felt comfort and companionship in reading her Bible, the only book she ensured was packed for this trip.

Because of macular degeneration, she had lost the ability to see its fine print but by turning her head aside and moving the book close to her face, she could see enough of the chapter names at the top of the pages and some of the verse numbers. From years of study, she knew the chapter narratives and many favorite verses by heart, quotes she had memorized as talismans to guide her.

On this morning, she flipped pages to Philippians 3-4; she smiled. Of course. Immediately, she visualized the words from verses 11-13. Brushing her hand over the words, she said aloud from memory:

"I am not saying this because I am in need, for I have learned to be content whatever the circumstances. I know what it is to be in need, and I know what it is to have plenty. I have learned the secret of being content in any and every situation, whether well-fed or hungry, whether living in plenty or in want. I can do everything through Him who gives me strength."

She reflected on the meaning. Ironically, since vocalizing her prayer to die, she felt relieved, a strange contentment; it was now in God's hands. She would not whine and snivel toward death; she would welcome it as she had requested it, and live each day fully until death came for her, and she knew it was coming soon because she had called it.

But, what to do with this day—with this long and blank day?

She knew a priority needed to be getting up and moving because some food from last night's dinner felt unsettled in her gut. The heavy gas bloated up into her chest. Moving should help.

"What makes me content?" She knew the answer before even finishing the thought. Gardening. Yes, gardening.

For hours she prepared, scavenging the house closets for old outdoor wear, clothing that no one would notice was worn and wet for one more time—a winter cap of Madeline's, a hooded rain jacket of John's, rain boots of Claire's, and a very old pair of wool working gloves from who knows whom and when.

Even with all her effort, the gas had not worked its way out but settled into an upper abdominal discomfort. She found and took some antacids from the bathroom cabinet. It was already noon. Time for lunch, but she wasn't hungry because preparing for an afternoon in the soil took away any appetite, but she had to eat something and settled on microwaving tomato soup. In lifting the spoon, her arm ached. "I must have pulled a muscle," she thought, recalling efforts from the previous day.

Two hours later, she stood at the garage door slightly out of breath, feeling a little out of sorts, and dressed for the elements in a hodge-podge of winter wear. Once in the garage, she fumbled and felt around, finding a shovel and an old metal rake.

With the tools for balance, she walked out the garage side door and through the back-fence gate into the backyard. Rain drizzled. Everything felt wet. She shivered. Walking over to the slab back porch, she noticed her left arm felt disconnected from her body, but anticipation for gardening silenced any concern before it could form into a warning. From years of gardening, she knew that once her hands were in the soil, so to speak, with rake or shovel, she would be content in any circumstance.

Carefully, with one steadied and balanced step after another, she stepped off the concrete slab and began walking the circumference of the yard, surveying her imagined project. "The humidity makes it so hard to breath," she said aloud, checking to see if she had the breath to say the words. A thin layer of leaves from a neighbor's oak tree and another's maple covered the ground. Laying the shovel against the fence and using the rake, she scraped the layers of wet leaves from a patch of uneven ground and saw what she had been searching for—the turned up soil under leaf mulch from her daughter's weekend attempt to prepare a patch for a garden. Rosemarie had remembered Claire telling her in one of their bi-monthly phone calls about her idea to plant a garden. Her heart raced at the find.

With pulls, tugs, and releases, she scraped leaves through grass sprouts and uneven sod. The falling mist softened the ground and made the effort easier, but her left arm tingled with numb-ness. Interesting. Pull, tap, pile, lift, return, pull, tap, pile, lift, return.

She paused and arched her back straight to

stretch. The drizzle tapped her face and she spoke up into the sky, again testing her capacity to breathe, "I will not plant vegetables," she caught her breath and balance and continued, "nothing utilitarian. Instead…flowers, bright and beautiful…to feed my soul." Each word required effort.

Although math had been her teaching specialty, she could still recite the right poem for the right moment, as her own mother had done throughout her life, and today in the cold drizzle, she recited into the moisture-laden air with an effort in the breath for each word, one of her favorite poems from the 13th century:

"If of thy mortal goods,….thou art bereft,
And from thy slender store….two loaves alone to thee are left,
Sell one,….and with the dole
Buy hyacinths….to feed thy soul."

The pronounced pauses for breath added drama to the moment, but strangely, in forming the word "hyacinths," her jaw ached.

"Hmm," she rolled her tongue in her mouth. "Hyacinths. Hyacinths. I've never felt this pain before." In a flash, in the millisecond before a life-saving insight connecting all the converging pains could finally form a warning, she lost the thought to fright at the sound of crunching leaves, human steps, directly behind her.

"Hi, Grandma." It was Madeline.

Rosemarie froze and her heart pounded, all before the voice registered as her granddaughter's. In the next seconds, she focused on regaining balance and breath, deep breaths, while leaning on the rake to avoid toppling over. She didn't have the reflexes she once had. With balance retained, she tried to take in several breaths, felt again startled by the lack of access to air and by the effort, and turned to greet her granddaughter.

"Gosh, I'm sorry I scared you," said Madeline, standing a few feet away. Rosemarie could only see the dark form of the rain jacket and hood and not the child within.

"Come here, child," she gasped out the words and lifted and opened her arm for an embrace. Madeline walked into the embrace. Madeline was her only granddaughter, and if any true blessing came from this time at her daughter's home, it was Madeline, the true remaining blessing.

Each summer since age five, Madeline had spent a week with her. Although exhausting, Rosemarie loved those weeks and planned each detail and participated in all activities knowing she would have time to recover after Madeline went home. She adored her granddaughter.

"How was….your day?" asked Rosemarie, pausing to inhale and to concentrate on breathing.

For a long moment Madeline did not respond, and then said, "Good."

After thirty years of teaching high school math, Rosemarie could recognize a child's lie in one word, in the tone, inflection, and cadence of just one, one-syllable word. It was a talent developed from teaching. Her granddaughter was lying, and not terribly skilled at it. However, teaching high school and raising a child of her own taught her not to interrogate but to wait and watch.

"Great," said Rosemarie, still struggling to breathe. "Love your help. Take this rake. Rake the leaves….We'll talk later."

Rosemarie stretched out her arm to transfer the rake. Madeline took the rake and turned to work. In the moment of this exchange as their faces passed within inches, Rosemarie saw something in the light of the exchange. What was it? What was it? It frightened her. She watched the form of Madeline walking away. Something was noticeably wrong, sensed in a second's exchange.

It wasn't what she had seen. It was what she had not seen. It was a lack of light, a void, a darkness. She felt it.

Rosemarie raced through thoughts about her granddaughter, trying to put logic to what just happened. This child always had such light, such unbridled curiosity and combustible energy. She exuded light. She is light.

Rosemarie grasped her chest, feeling the full force of the discomfort—a squeezing pain burning through her chest to her back and converging as a weight that wouldn't let her breathe. She stumbled to the plastic lawn chair on the concrete slab porch, grabbed the shovel, and used it to help her sit on the wet plastic. How could she have been so self-absorbed not to have noticed until now? HOW! She wanted to scream, but she had no breath. How could she have missed it?

With the squeezing moving into searing pain, Rosemarie focused on her granddaughter. For Rosemarie, a remarkable gift, one she had never spoken about, grew as her eyesight faded, and now this gift showed her something that absolutely and completely terrified her.

"No, No, No!" her thoughts screamed.

Rosemarie had the ability when she cared and

really concentrated, or sometimes in unwelcome sparks, to see the light energy surrounding each person. Each person's light energy flashed and moved and swirled from the person's own being, and this light responded to the energy from others and from the environment in that moment. At its best, in moments of joy, a person's light exploded and danced like the aurora borealis, bringing forth the colors, and rhythms, and patterns of that exact energy exchange, bringing forth the colors of the soul.

Now with her chest constricting and fighting unbearable pain, she concentrated on bringing the backdrop to the foreground and seeing what she should have seen a week ago when she arrived. How could she have been so blind!?

Madeline, whose back was turned, slowly raked the leaves. Rosemarie focused on her—truly terrified. Soon the form of Madeline faded and her lights—the child's own aura—sparked in the forefront. Rosemarie gasped and she closed her eyes as she saw what she feared was true. Madeline's lights did not dance. They did not shoot and dart and expand and explode into the colors of the rainbow. Instead, they sputtered and barely hummed. The child's spirit, her own divine light, was fading. The light barely lit her form, and darkness encroached upon her, like a black hole, into the absence of light.

Instinctively, Rosemarie reached out for her granddaughter, but her arm would not move. She focused on her arm and the full force of the pain. "It feels like childbirth in my chest," she thought, and might have laughed at the image had she not recognized at that moment what the pain was bringing. Death. It was coming. It was coming now, and it was coming too soon!

"Not now!" her thoughts pleaded. From somewhere in the whirlwind of pain and distress, she vaguely recalled, "Didn't I invite death to come?"

With force, she fell hard onto the concrete patio. Pain exploded from her heart into every cell of her body. It zipped through her extremities, and then nothing.

She felt nothing. Seconds later, for the first time in months, she felt warm. She rested in the warmth, relieved. It felt good. The warmth calmed her, lulling her to sleep. But she wasn't asleep; she could see herself below. She was watching herself sprawled out on the patio as from an overhead camera shot from a movie. She watched. With detachment and complete comfort and peace, she watched her granddaughter run over, fall on her knees next to her sprawled body, shout at her, shake her, check her mouth, and then with locked arms bang her palms, over and over hard into her chest.

"Interesting," she thought, feeling nothing.

Then, as part of the same detached and silent movie, her granddaughter fumbled with her cell phone, called someone, shouted something, threw the cell phone down, and returned to banging on her chest.

Rosemarie watched. No pain. No rush. No need to interrupt the scene below her. She felt content, at great peace and warmth and comfort, puzzled by all the commotion. In the back of her mind, she knew something had disturbed her moments before, but she couldn't remember what it was. "What was it?"

The answer formed at the same time she realized what her granddaughter was doing. "YOU CAN DO IT! YOU MUST SAVE ME!" Rosemarie screamed from her viewpoint above, and from the energy of the plea, she witnessed her own lips move, barely, but they moved. Madeline noticed this too. She bent over the lips of her grandmother and screamed something Rosemarie could not hear, but she knew the child's efforts were not working. The child waited for the response, which was no response, and then in a movement of inspiration, she took in a deep and long breath, grabbed her grandmother's jaw and forehead, sealed her own lips to hers and blew.

From the soul-wresting detachment, Rosemarie felt her granddaughter's cold lips on her own, and felt the forceful breaths flood into her body with ear piercing sound: "Yah, Yah, Yah."

A dam blocking her air's passage broke, and air flowed into her like ice water. In the pain, Rosemarie gasped, "Wehhhhhhhh!" She gasped again, "Yahhhhhhhhh." And, then a third time with joy, "Wehhhhhhh."

"Grandma!" Madeline screamed looking over her and gasping for air, "You are alive!"

Rosemarie shivered, now back in her body. She took in more cold and deep breaths, thankful for each one. The breaths hurt. Her chest hurt; her arm hurt; her body felt wet with cold sweat, and her back felt frozen on the concrete.

"Grandma, you are alive!" Madeline said again.

"Yes," Rosemarie said, struggling to speak against the pain flooding back into her.

"The ambulance is on the way. I think you had a heart attack."

"Yes," Rosemarie said, grabbing her granddaughter's arm. She had to act fast.

"The ambulance should be here in a moment," Madeline said.

"Honey, I need...." Rosemarie struggled to form her thoughts and words. She didn't have much time. "I need you to keep this a secret."

"A secret?" Madeline said looking frightened and confused.

"Child, listen," Rosemarie spoke in starts of breaths and fits of shivering. "If you tell...your mother... I had a heart attack...she will move me to a nursing home...You know this." She groaned from the cold and the pain of the effort.

"Let me get a blanket."

"No, listen. You need....Do NOT tell your mother. We will tell her later.... There's something I must do first."

"Grandma, it will be impossible to keep this a secret," Madeline said in a tone Rosemarie recognized.

"Madeline, I'm not crazy....Trust me. Do

this...for me. It's essential." Rosemarie heard the sirens coming up the street.

"Grandma, listen to the sirens! How can we keep this a secret! The entire neighborhood will hear this."

"Calm down. Listen," Rosemarie used a tone she had never used with Madeline, only with delinquent students. She didn't have the energy or breath for an argument. The questioning was over. "YOU don't know your neighbors. THEY don't know you...NO ONE CARES... not enough to tell your mother. No one will notice."

"Grandm...," Madeline started to interrupt.

"No! The ambulance...here. Let them in...Get my purse....Go to the hospital with me....Act with authority. Be smart."

"Grandma, Mom is going to kill me!"

Rosemarie squeezed her hand. "With luck...she won't notice...At the hospital...give them my insurance card...in my purse...If we can pay, no one will ask."

Bang. Bang. Bang. "Paramedics!"

"Honey," Rosemarie squeezed her granddaughter's hand, "You saved me. Now you can do this....I am counting on you. Trust me....You MUST, absolutely must, keep this secret. Do I have your word?"

Madeline nodded yes, and Rosemarie relaxed into the searing pain.

Chapter 7
Madeline's Problem

Madeline ran through the house with cell phone in hand, flung open the door, nodded at the paramedics with backpacks and a stretcher, turned, and led them to the backyard.

"What happened?" asked the tall, lanky one jogging behind her.

"Grandma quit breathing. I think she had a heart attack."

"Is she breathing now?" asked the short, stout man.

"She is now," said Madeline just as they arrived at the back porch.

She stepped to the side and let them pass.

Both knelt on either side of Grandma and began their work. Madeline brought the cell phone to her ear. Her hand shook. "They are here."

"Good," said the 911 operator. "She is very lucky you were with her."

Madeline tried to think of a reply and simply said, "Thank you."

"I will hang up now," said the voice. "Good work, young lady."

In the seconds of that exchange, the paramedics had moved Grandma onto a stretcher, placed an oxygen mask on her face, unbuttoned the jacket, cut open her sweater, and set up an IV. While the burly paramedic asked her grandmother "yes" and "no" questions, to which she nodded, the tall one poked the IV needle into her arm and taped it down.

Madeline shivered. Sweat from terror and action had soaked all of her clothes within the raincoat shell.

"What?" Grandma lifted her arm and mumbled something through the oxygen mask.

"Relax ma'm. If your ECG indicates a heart blockage—we'll need the IV to administer a cocktail of reteplase and heparin. One's a clot buster and the other a blood thinner," replied the tall paramedic.

Madeline watched the paramedics work with choreographed movements, like the same scene rehearsed a thousand times to a different backdrop. The stout guy pulled out and organized colored wires from a box inside the backpack, pulled off sticky tags at the end of the wires and attached them to her grandmother's chest and side. He spoke through each action: "It's a tele-electrocardiography system; we'll be transmitting your ECG using this cell phone hookup, and the emergency room should be ready when we arrive."

"What is your name?" the tall paramedic asked Madeline without taking his eyes off his work.

"Madeline."

"My name is Jarrod. And, Madeline, you're shivering. How about you go inside, put on some dry clothes, and then come back."

"No!" came the muffled shout of Grandma.

"Stay calm," the tall paramedic rubbed her shoulder. "She'll be right back."

Madeline did as instructed as quickly as she could. When she returned, Grandma motioned for her to come to her. She stood over her and was about to bend down when the stout man said, "Jarrod, we're ready to roll." He pushed a button on the transmitter attached to his arm and spoke into it. "She's stable, hooked up, and transmitting, and we're transporting now. Over."

"We are receiving the data. See you in 20," replied the voice through the transmitter.

Jarrod stood with a leap, put on his backpack of supplies, grabbed one side of the stretcher, and motioned for Madeline to step back. "One, two, three, lift," he said, and the stretcher rose like an ironing board.

Madeline stood next to the stretcher.

"Get my purse," said Grandma.

Madeline found the purse in the guest room next to Grandma's open Bible.

She rushed to the front door. Grandma was trying to take her mask off. The stout paramedic was holding it on and trying to comfort her.

"Madeline, come here," motioned Jarrod. She checked for the keys in her jean pocket, locked the front door, and rushed over to the ambulance.

"Your grandmother says she won't be transported unless you're with her," said Jarrod.

"I'm here."

"Stand back a moment, Madeline," said

Jarrod, and as she did, the men pushed the stretcher forward, and the rolling stand compacted and Grandma slid smoothly into the ambulance. Jarrod grabbed a rail, swung himself up, and began securing parts into place.

"You can ride up here with me," said the stout paramedic to Madeline.

"No," came Grandma's emphatic and mumbled response. "She will ride back with me!"

Jarrod looked at the stout man who shrugged.

"Stan, she'll be fine in the back," said Jarrod.

He then turned to Madeline, smiled, and offered his hand to help her up. "Yes, you can help me. Get in here."

Madeline took Jarrod's hand, which enveloped hers, and he pulled her up into the ambulance. He then pulled down a rumble seat from the wall across from him and next to Grandma's shoulder. Stan shut the door and banged on it twice.

"It's good luck," said Jarrod, flashing a smile.

Stan drove the ambulance without a siren, and Jarrod checked electronic monitors while speaking to the hospital on his shoulder transmitter.

"The ST portion of the ECG is showing a STEMI," said the voice speaking back.

"ETA is 17 minutes," said Jarrod.

"The cardio cath lab will be ready when you arrive. We're assembling the team now," said the voice.

"Madeline," said Grandma, reaching out and touching her.

Madeline quit listening to the medical conversation and focused on her.

"Listen, child," she said, reaching her hand over her mouth, taking off her mask and holding it on her chin. Madeline looked at Jarrod. He said nothing and continued to monitor the equipment and talk to the medical staff.

"It appears," she said quietly, and Madeline had to lean in to hear her, "I have a blocked artery to my heart. When we arrive...Did you bring my purse?"

"Yes."

"After they check my insurance, I will be having a procedure—an angioplasty."

Madeline noticed her concentrating with tremendous focus to speak, forcing air into her lungs and speaking during the exhale.

"The doctors will insert a tube," she paused for breath. "It has an inflatable balloon. It will open my clogged artery."

"Heart surgery?" Madeline said, more to herself.

"Listen. It's routine. But," and taking a deep breath, she emphasized, "your mother CANNOT know about this."

Madeline could not believe she was still blabbering about this.

"If your mother finds out, I will be in a nursing home. She will do it."

Her words were true. Madeline knew this. But, keeping this a secret!

"Grandma, you will be in the hospital for days. For starters, how am I supposed to hide your absence at dinner tonight?" Madeline looked at Jarrod.

Jarrod gave Madeline a questioning look that indicated he had heard, but he continued to monitor the electronic device in front of him and to provide information to the voice speaking from the transmitter on his shoulder.

"Stay calm," Grandma whispered and spoke between breaths. "Listen, Uncle Stan had this done. I was there. It takes 40 minutes tops. Easy."

"But you can't just get off the operating table and come home! It's already near dinner. Mom gets home by 5:30 at the latest. I bet you're in the hospital at least until tomorrow."

"Okay," said Grandma. "Check me in." She paused and took in a breath after each phrase. "With my insurance card, no one will question. Get money from my purse. Take a cab. You can make it home by 5:30. Look calm. Take my purse with you."

"How is this LIE going to work?"

"Listen, you will not lie. I don't want you to lie. You will omit. You can omit. Just don't say anything about this."

"Mom doesn't notice much, but she will notice you missing from dinner tonight!"

Grandma was breathing more easily now, able to speak with less effort.

"Okay, I've got it. At the hospital, have Jarrod give us one minute outside before he wheels me in. I'll call your mother on her cell phone. Hopefully she won't pick up, and I can leave a message. I'll tell her that..." Grandma paused, obviously thinking of the plan as she spoke, "Tom and Mary Jane are passing through town; they invited me to dinner and to stay with them in their timeshare for a day or two." She paused, thought, and said, "You need to hide my suit case."

"What!?"

"It will work. Trust me."

Madeline looked away, shaking her head.

"Madeline," Grandma said, pulling her back. "This must work until I do what I've been brought back to do."

"What? What do you mean, brought back to…?"

"Promise me!" she interrupted with a command.

Madeline sighed, stalling in a long, deep breath. In that breath, she knew that her response, like no decision she had ever made before, would somehow change everything, and not in ways she could predict or control. This was a huge risk— she could hear her mother's voice say "a great lack of judgment and responsibility." She felt the weight in these words and in the request; and she knew the consequences could be dire, and in the same breath, she knew there was only one answer.

"I promise. I will keep your secret."

Chapter 8
Claire's Responsibilities

Claire felt relieved that her mother had been invited to spend a few nights with old friends at their timeshare. She always liked Tom and Mary Jane, and her mother in her phone message sounded excited to be seeing them. She sounded tired too, which reminded Claire that she needed to find a long-term solution for her mother's care, but not tonight. Thank God she didn't have to worry about this tonight.

Instead, she could worry about paying the bills. "What an unusual evening," Claire thought as she prepared the dining room table for the task: stacking the debit receipts, plugging in the portable computer with the budget software, retrieving the backup calculator from a kitchen drawer, accessing the banking account online, printing out the debit charges, and pulling out the check register from her wallet. She organized the space; it felt good to have order with something.

Dinner had felt strained. Claire believed in the family eating dinner together. She had read somewhere that this one event resulted in children who were more stable. Therefore, every night as close to 6:00 p.m. as possible, she had some form of dinner on the table, usually created from a combination of thawed portions of frozen fish or meat, frozen vegetables, and a microwaved starch. With Mom and John gone, tonight she ate alone with Madeline, who—well, quite frankly—was not behaving like herself. She wondered about the hitchhiker and what influence he had on her daughter. Claire had decided not to question her about this until after the counselor appointment, which left little else to talk about.

Madeline seemed nervous, jumpy almost, and whenever Claire tried to ask her a question, she interrupted with a question of her own, and appeared to be riveted in the answer. And, although Claire enjoyed sharing about herself, answering questions that ranged from how strict her own mother was to if her family had a history of heart disease, something did not feel right. It felt forced, but soon Claire realized her daughter simply didn't want to talk about the hitchhiker. That was it for sure. So, she played along and did not let on that she knew.

Madeline excused herself to go study in her room, and Claire focused on reconciling the bank ledger to the check carbons and debit receipts. Someday soon she resolved to start saving postage and paying her bills online, but so far, she didn't have the time or the energy to set up the service, so she paid through the mail.

First, she recorded the mortgage payment. This reminded her that their house had lost 30 percent of its value in the last three years, and they owed more than the house was worth. The realization stopped her for one breath, in and out of silent reflection, which passed in the next breath with the acknowledgment that she could pay for one more month. Next, she wrote checks for and recorded the amounts for the recurring bills—home electricity, car gas, cable television, phone service, cell phone, home insurance, car insurance, internet, etc. Then, as quickly as she could, she stacked the debit receipts in order by date, reviewed the list of debit charges with dates John had emailed yesterday, wrote each on a separate slip of scratch paper, and placed each in order by date within her pile of debits. Then, she recorded each of these in the software register. Like every month before, her actions were mechanical— unimportant details organized into an assembly line—but a familiar accompanying anxiety reminded her about the importance of one lost or excessive detail.

She paused before recording the debit charge for John's rent. She would have to cash another one of Madeline's college bonds to pay for the next few months of his rent and then just hope that his future income could replace their original savings. She believed in this plan once, this plan for the future. But, with each debit she recorded, she began to question if they could ever build back the college savings plan. Their retirement accounts had still not recovered from the last market crash, and they most likely would need Madeline's college money to fund their retirement. Claire tapped her pen on the table and contemplated the financial tightrope of their future. Everything had to go well—as planned—for their plan to work, and nothing in life seemed to go as planned.

The grocery bills, house heating, and car gas bills had gone up noticeably in the last year. She could see this even before she checked the register entries against the bank statement and then totaled the amount. She would have to find another expense to cut. Two candidates, which she had been holding in a mental cue, came forward in her thoughts: the phone landline or the cable TV.

The phone rang, and Claire didn't mind the distraction. "I'll get it," she yelled back to Madeline, who hopefully was studying as she promised.

"Hi," Claire said, seeing on the caller I.D. that it was John.

"I'm sorry I didn't call last night," said John. "I had a night class until 9:00, and when I checked my messages after class, it was like 11:00 your time, and I knew you were in bed. What happened with Madeline?"

Claire lowered her voice, cupped her hand around the mouthpiece, and whispered. "She denies anything happened, but I called Dr. Hancock anyway, and she is scheduled to see him Thursday."

"When we're finished, let me talk with her,

hon, but first, tell me exactly what happened," said John.

Claire turned on the kitchen radio, returned her hand cupped around the phone, and felt contained emotions surfacing. She explained how she found Madeline cavorting with a hitchhiker on a known route for interstate travel. She shared every detail she knew, which led to a summary of Madeline's punishment, and then to the need to start investigating nursing homes for Rosemarie, and next to her struggles with the board in finalizing her most recent work grant—the one she needed to review one more time after finishing the bills tonight. This led to an unloading about their dwindling financial situation. Each topic stirred the waves of her emotions. She saved all the emotional details for these calls with John, often telling herself before his calls that she would restrain and not burden him, but always her emotional dam broke, and the feelings flooded from her.

Toward the end of 30 minutes, she just stopped talking, spent from the effort. She'd said it all. John had listened. The flood had passed, swept through. He was a good listener. He was a good man.

Then, with her energy spent, the conversation tacked, and John led. He shared about test scores, contacts, and job possibilities for graduates. He offered hope.

Claire listened and relaxed into the soothing rhythm of his words, in a speech she knew and trusted. He made her laugh. She breathed in the moment and drifted, soothed in the flow. For a few moments, she forgot about her budget and her grant reviews. She forgot about her chores, and she forgot about the gap between her life and her plans. She simply let John guide them through the moments.

When she finally let go and completely relaxed into a moment, she felt the soul searing exhaustion rise up and ooze from every muscle and shattered nerve. John was the eye of her storm, and in his presence she could rest and feel disappointed and tired of trying.

"Hon, I think it is a little after 9:00 your time," John finally said. "You should get Madeline. I should probably talk to her now before she gets ready for bed."

Claire agreed and called, "Maddie, your dad wants to talk to you." Usually, such a call resulted in the instantaneous burst of Madeline from behind her bedroom door. But, she did not respond. Claire called again. Her heart beat quickened, and she snapped back into stress mode.

"John, give me a minute," she said, putting down the phone and walking back to Madeline's bedroom with dread. She slowly opened the door. Madeline was not in her room. A bright study lamp lit an open book. Silence.

On alert, Claire quickly checked each room. Through the window in the guest bedroom, she saw a flicker of a human figure in the backyard. Her heart jumped from alert to terror before her brain recognized the figure as Madeline in her winter coat standing on the back porch looking up into the darkness.

Anger now replaced terror, "What is wrong with this child!?" she yelled.

She stormed through the doors from the house to the garage and from the garage to the backyard gate.

Madeline turned. Claire stopped. Her daughter looked tired, very tired and distant. Madeline smiled slightly, with a look not recognizing the rage that arrived with her mother. Claire felt confused and blasted both by her daughter and the cold. She didn't speak. She had forgotten why she went looking for Madeline.

"Mom?"

"Yes?"

Madeline looked and pointed up to the night sky. Claire followed her finger and looked up. The rain clouds had cleared, and amidst a few wisps of white and against a dark night Venus flickered with a few other dots of light.

"The stars are beautiful, aren't they?" said Madeline.

Claire didn't know what to say. She watched her daughter.

"Mom?" Madeline said still looking up at the sky.

"Yes," Claire said with some edge this time. She wasn't amused in the slightest. She didn't have time for this.

"Do you believe in God?"

"What?

"Do you believe God answers our prayers?"

"What?" Claire said, more scared for her daughter now than angry.

"Grandma believes. She believes that God answers prayers."

"Honey," Claire said with as much patience as she could muster, "What are you doing out here? I'm freezing."

Madeline looked down from the sky, looked at her mother, and said softly, "Mom, I am looking for my prayer."

Claire felt the deep chill of fear, far deeper than the chill of that night. "Well," she said trying not to show her concern, "you need to look for your prayer inside and later because your dad is on the phone and he wants to speak with you."

Madeline raced past her mother, and seconds later, Claire heard her yell, "Hi, Daddy!"

Claire stood on the cold, dark porch. She looked up, spotting Venus, lighting the outline of clouds through the darkness. The sweat on her back turned cold. It took her breath away. Shivering, she waited a moment. She focused on catching her breath from the frigid air and expelling it in visible puffs. She needed to say something. With her breath back, she spoke into the darkness:

"Thank God I scheduled that psychologist appointment for her."

Chapter 9
Madeline's Responsibilities

The secret awoke Madeline. Before the light, before the alarm, before the impossibility of it all returned, it simply woke her. Wide awake, she felt different than yesterday and different than the day before. "Better"—the thought flashed. "Why?" No answer came to her, but she knew—she had a problem to solve, and it was bigger than her own problems.

Then, within seconds, reason flooded with anxiety from the impossibility of it all and from the for-sure-resulting trouble of it all. She felt her heart beating rapidly, as if she had just run a mile, but all she had done was open her eyes and look

at the ceiling. She reviewed what had happened
the night before and hoped a better plan might
emerge.

Last night after dinner during feigned study
time, she called the hospital receptionist, learned
Grandma's room number, and called the room.
When Grandma didn't answer, she called the
receptionist back and was transferred to the floor
nurse. The floor nurse shared that Grandma had
made it through the surgery successfully and that
she was resting in ICU for a few more hours
before being transferred to her hospital room.

She had to make a plan to get her home. The
first plan involved pretending to go to school,
skipping school, taking the bus across town, and
getting to the hospital to get her home. No. The
school would call her mother. The next plan
involved disguising her voice as her mother and
calling in sick. She practiced in a whisper. She still
sounded nothing like her mother, but after a while
she thought maybe she sounded a little like her.
She tested the imitation by recording her voice
using the cell message recorder. Playing it back,
she clearly heard her voice, young and shaky. No.
She worked through a dozen plans like this, some
so ridiculous she rolled her own eyes at them.

With all plans reviewed and dismissed, long after the lights were out and long after midnight, Madeline was exhausted from the effort, but she had settled on an approach rather than a plan— the one she arrived at again this next morning. To protect her grandma's secret, she would attend school, at least until she could escape unnoticed and then get to the hospital to bring her home safely and secretly. Somehow and someway, with really no idea how, she would figure out the details along the way.

School felt surreal. For the first time since starting junior high months ago, she felt relieved to be invisible. Before the start of first period, she walked the morning gauntlet to her locker. Surrounded by the familiar blasts of banging lockers, shrills of laughing and jockeying girls, and baritones of boys jostling and joking, she walked alone and did not feel lonely. No one noticed. She simply watched and waited for an opportunity.

After retrieving her books from her locker, she saw Katie, a friend from grade school, opening her locker. She noticed for the first time how Katie didn't try to contribute to the commotion or cower from its blast, but she seemed to stand apart. Katie didn't rush in fearful motions or look around for someone's approval or try to fade into her locker or into the walls or into anything stable and strong. Instead, she moved with a quiet confidence, completely overshadowed by the rush and noise around her and detectable in the contrast by graceful movements uniquely her own.

Madeline walked past the rows of lockers. "Hi Katie."

Katie turned and her eyes smiled. "Hi Maddie. Which way are you walking to homeroom?"

Madeline pointed to the right, and Katie replied, "Me too." The noise and rush faded into background. "Maddie, my mom signed me up for Smart Reading, you know the Saturday program. We read to pre-school kids at the library by your house. Would you like to come some Saturday?"

"Sure. I would love to help."

The walk was too short to her homeroom but long enough to make a new friend from an old friend and long enough to matter.

First period math sucked the life out of the previous connection. She couldn't concentrate, and she hated this math class.

In sixth grade, Madeline had loved math, and enjoyed it all grades before this. She loved her sixth grade math teacher, Mrs. Grey, the energy in the class, and the feeling of accomplishment at getting the right answer. Problems were riddles to be solved, everyone participated, and each student signed a contract to help other students learn. They were Mrs. Grey's math team!

Now, because of her average scores on a standardized placement test, she placed into an average class with an average teacher, Mr. Bates. He taught using what he called on the first day "a self-paced method" because this "allowed for individual success." Madeline didn't notice success. She noticed each student faced the computer screen quietly clicking away, and Mr. Bates sat at his desk facing the classroom while reading his magazines, only rising when someone called him for assistance. To earn an A, she had to successfully complete 40 online packets. She learned quickly how to successfully complete an online packet and its test for the A. Now, on most days, stuck in class and going through the motions to earn an A, she daydreamed about being in the other math class.

A few weeks ago, during a bathroom break, she passed the open door to the other math class for the students who excelled on the placement test—the "gifted" students. She stopped and watched from an angle least likely to be noticed. Inside, each student stood in front of a whiteboard working on an assigned problem. Turning in a semi-circle in the center of the room was the teacher, a man, speaking in excited tones and with urgency. "Ben, you got it. That's it. Sarah, that is it too. Good job. Wow, Tessa that is a unique way to solve the problem, and it is correct. Everyone look at Tessa's approach." Students stopped and gathered around the girl. Several tapped her on the shoulder, a few gave her high fives, and others surrounded her to study her answer.

"Okay, back to work," guided the teacher. A moment later he paused at the whiteboard of a tall, thin boy. "James, you got the same type of problem right 10 minutes ago. You know it. Look for the error." They both stood staring at the board. Madeline stared too. She saw the error and in excitement wanted to say something, and then froze knowing she was not a part of the class.

"You know it," encouraged the teacher. "John, take a look and show us." Another boy walked over, looked at the whiteboard, and said. "Oh, see the x squared." Immediately James jumped with his marker to fix the mistake.

"Good," said the teacher. "Now, let's try this one." He clicked the remote in his hand and on a wall displayed a new problem. Students erased their previous answers while the teacher said, "This is an example of a simple force equation. You will be using these equations in physics class in a few years to determine the functionality of a bridge—to determine if it will bear your car safely over it."

"I just want a car; forget the bridge," said James.

"How about a 1968 Mustang," said John.

"No, no, no," said Sarah. "You want an electric hybrid, really."

Several students laughed; others joined in the chatter, all started working on the new problem.

Madeline watched. A boy in the class noticed her watching, appeared used to an audience, looked through her with no emotion, turned his back to the door and faced his equation. He said into the chatter, "I'm not picky—I'll take any of those cars."

Madeline wished she had scored smart enough to be in that class. Instead, on this morning, the contrast of this memory against the repetitive sound of computer clicks and keyboard

taps from students solving their individual packets of math problems reminded her second by
second, tap by tap, that she needed to be somewhere else, and she had no idea how to get there.

At the classroom buzzer, Madeline logged off
the computer and raced to the lunchroom with her
backpack. When she opened the lunchroom door,
four other girls and two boys glanced up at her
anxiously, saw it was just another student, and
went back to text messaging in their own corners
of the dimly lit room. School rules prohibited any
cell phone use during school hours, but everyone
knew that the rule was not enforced as long as it
occurred in between class, no adult noticed, and
all offenders made it to class on time.

Taking the phone from the backpack pocket,
she flipped off mute and dialed the hospital number by tapping "recent." She waited for the operator and asked to be connected to the cardiac
recovery nurses' station. A man answered, and
she asked about the status of her grandma in room
415. "Let me check," he said. A few long minutes
later, the voice said, "She is sleeping and doing
well."

"When can she go home?"

"Let me see," said the man, obviously

checking something. "Who are you?" he asked a moment later.

"I'm her granddaughter."

"Okay, well it shows here that we are preparing the release papers right now, and Dr. Andert will be making her rounds about 1:00 this afternoon. Your grandmother could be released as early as this afternoon or it might be another day. I really can't say. The doctor and your grandmother will decide."

Madeline said nothing. After several seconds of silence, the man added, "But kid, don't worry. I spoke with your grandmother this morning, and she is doing well. The surgery went well. She's a determined lady."

"Thank you," said Madeline, hanging up and muting her cell phone, stuffing it into the backpack, and hurrying to the next class.

The next class was history, and Mrs. Jacobson gave the students a lecture-free period to brainstorm ideas for their history papers and to search school-approved websites for sources. Having already determined the purpose of her paper, Madeline uploaded her previously prepared notes and searched the internet for Civil War battlegrounds. She clicked from link to link, appearing fully engaged while using the computer as a facade while determining how to implement an escape plan.

She needed to be at the hospital by 1:00, which meant planning a way to leave school at lunch unnoticed. Also, she had forgotten about the money to transport Grandma home. The bus would require too many stops and steps and standing. She didn't have enough money for a taxi, and she had left Grandma's purse under her bed at home.

Mrs. Jacobson walked the rows and stopped to help students with questions. Madeline re-typed a few of her thoughts from the top of her notes to appear adequately busy. After copying a line, she paused, studied the computer screen, tried to appear thoughtful, and then copied another line. She knew Mrs. Jacobson wasn't close enough to see the words.

One problem stumped Madeline. During school hours, all doors, except the school's front doors, were activated as emergency exits. She could exit one of these emergency exit doors, but this action would trigger a buzzer in the administrative office and would trip on the surveillance cameras associated with the door. They would see her. Her only chance of escaping unseen had to involve walking out the front door, by the administrative office, by the principal's office, by the secretary, and by the security guard.

She imagined crawling, running, darting, rolling, and all other forms of movement. No. One of them would see her. She imagined again faking a call from her mother to the school. No. Faking a note? No. Faking a call from her father? Maybe, but who could be her father? The hitchhiker. Yes. She had his business card somewhere. He would understand.

The class bell rang. Madeline jumped. She canceled the fake history notes, logged off the computer, grabbed her binder, and ran out of the classroom. She needed to check her backpack in her locker for the business card that she had transferred from her pocket, and in case this did not work, check her escape route before the start of her next class—her last class before lunch.

Racing through the crowds, oblivious to whom she bumped or might insult, she opened her locker and searched. There in the backpack's mini-pocket was the business card with a URL but no phone number. This could be a problem unless the website has a phone number, but, first things first. She slipped the card into the binder for the next class and headed for the administrative offices.

When she reached the offices, her heart beat hard in her chest and up into her neck, and throbbed in her ears. Intentionally dropping her binder and scattering paper, she slowly bent down to pick up the mess, scanning the hall and the main doors. As she watched, a mother walked out of the window-lined administrative offices with her son and out the main doors. With the doors open, Madeline felt a strong, cold wind and noticed it was raining hard. None of her class-rooms had windows. Then, less than a minute later, another woman and a girl appearing ill walked out of the office and out the main door. The cold, wet wind blew through the hall.

"That's it," she thought. "I will tag behind another parent and child and blend in with them like I am part of their family. No one is watching that closely when the kids leave with parents." The buzzer rang for first warning for her next class, and she dashed back to class.

Now, 20 more minutes passed, and with 20 minutes left until lunch, she tried to concentrate on Mrs. Colby's directions and simultaneously imagine each step of her escape, but her heart banged up into her throat and ears and all she could focus on was her escape.

"Madeline, what did you find?" Mrs. Colby asked.

Madeline startled and bumped her binder, which plopped onto the floor, and banged her knee on her computer desk. It hurt. She gasped in a breath, reached down to pick up the binder, and tried to think about what the question could have been. Several computer printouts littered the floor, and Madeline moved quickly to pick them up.

Mrs. Colby, the English teacher whom Madeline genuinely liked for her kindness, gave her time to think while rephrasing the question. "Madeline," the sound of her voice smiled, "When you pulled up the three different homepages, each one prepared by a different constituent or stake-holder, about the same topic, what distinctions did you notice?"

With the papers picked up, Madeline saw the business card with the URL from the hitchhiker now on the floor next to her foot. She picked it up and sat up to answer. "The first site wanted to sell something." She breathed in deeply. "The second site seemed more unbiased." She breathed out,

"And the third site contained someone's opinions."

"Okay, good," said Mrs. Colby. "Now, class, what are the site indicators that differentiate between selling, unbiased information, and opinions?"

Students began stating the indicators. Mrs. Colby walked to the board, made three columns, and began listing the indicators in their appropriate columns.

Madeline looked at the hitchhiker's URL on the business card in her hand. She knew the school rules, and until using her cell phone today, she fit into them compliantly, invisible without complaint. She was not allowed to visit or search any non-school sanctioned website during school hours or she would face expulsion. Each computer monitor displayed a sticker shouting in bold, all capped letters, "FOR SCHOOL USE ONLY."

"Type in this URL," Mrs. Colby said as she wrote out a new website address on the board.

Madeline positioned her hands to type the URL displayed on the board; instead, she typed the URL from the hitchhiker's card. She could feel this big mistake as she typed each letter, and she paused before hitting enter. She watched the key.

Her heart beat boomed.

"Okay, what do you see?" said Mrs. Colby.

Madeline looked up at Mrs. Colby. She was a teacher who mattered; she cared and tried and noticed her students. She smiled at Madeline. Madeline looked down. She stuffed the hitch-hiker's card into her pocket. She would not check it today.

The bell rang. Madeline grabbed her binder and notes and ran out of the classroom. She didn't have much time. As she raced to her locker, she stopped in mid-run feeling deep dread. For a second, she debated whether to lose precious time and go back to the classroom. She had forgotten to log out and most important to delete the hitch-hiker's URL out of the browser bar. No, she decided. She had to help her grandmother, and she didn't have much time if she hoped to help her and in doing so, keep the secret and the promise. The next student would log out for her.

She would not go back.

Chapter 10
Rosemarie's Responsibilities

Rosemarie could not rest. In the hours after being moved from the ICU and into her hospital bed as she faded in and out of consciousness, she was acutely aware of two things: her entire body ached and Madeline is in trouble. The first fact lured her toward sleep and the second jolted her awake.

With a soreness radiating through her chest and up her back and making each breath a conscious act, with arthritis aching in her hands, and with utter exhaustion and lingering anesthetic dulling any complaint, she pulled herself up using the side rails and focused all effort on staying upright, just one moment at a time. Breathe. Seconds passed. The dizziness subsided. Madeline is in trouble.

Careful not to dislodge the IV in her arm or any of the stuck-on pads connected to chest-monitoring wires, she shimmied slowly down to the foot of the bed toward the space between the end of the side rail and the footboard. With each shimmy, she inched the wheeled portable IV pole alongside the bed, ensuring that no wires and IV lines dislodged to signal her movement. Madeline is in trouble.

Finally, maneuvering her feet over the edge of the bed, she slid them down to the floor and slowly stood, balancing with one hand on the bedrail and the other on the IV pole. Her chest ached with each breath. Her hands ached. Her feet ached. Her head ached. Madeline is in trouble.

For reasons not clear to her, pushing the wheeled pole, she shuffled to the large window. From the corner of her eye, she could see her reflection in the window. She did not want to focus on how tired she must look, so she focused through her reflection. Outside billows of dark, heavy clouds churned in the turbulent sky. Rain pelted the window and joined to form streams racing sideways across the glass. Madeline is in trouble.

The knowledge had stirred her, but now as she looked out into the storm, she felt helpless to do anything. What can I do?

Feeling unbalanced by the frail and mobile support of the pole, she reached her other hand up against the window. A coldness transferred from the glass into her hand and through her body. She shivered, looked at her hand on the window, and then caught the glimpse of her reflected face touching it. She looked old. She looked exhausted. She looked scared. "Madeline is in trouble," she said into the glass. She felt old and helpless, and from the depths of this despair, she called out for help.

"God, I do not know what to do," she said, watching her reflection in the window. "My granddaughter is hurting; something is killing her spirit. I need to help her, and I do not know what to do. Madeline is in trouble. Please guide me. Please help me." The words "please help me" hung on and echoed into the room.

In her next thought, through exhaustion and clarity, she realized getting out of bed and walking unassisted to the window had taken all her strength. Right now it seemed like a bad idea, a very bad idea. Unsteady and weak, she knew it was time to get back into bed and quickly.

Inching her hand for balance along the cold window, she began to turn and transfer more weight onto the mobile pole, as she turned her head, she saw another reflected image in the window, and she gasped. It was both beautiful and absolutely terrifying. It? Her?

In the window she saw the image of an ancient woman. Her skin shone translucent and brown with wrinkles deep, long, and solid, like photos she had seen of Hopi elders. The woman's white and grey hair fell long and straight down her back over a light-brown robe, and disappeared beyond her waist. Her deep brown eyes filled the space around her with light, and they radiated a deep smile to Rosemarie, who felt warmed in the welcome.

Forgetting balance and exhaustion, Rosemarie turned away from the window and toward the room to her visitor. It took a few seconds to turn, and before she could reconnect with her guest's face and form, she felt the image move to her side and gently grasp her around the waist with confidence and strength, guiding her body.

"Okay, it's time to get you into bed," said the young voice.

The voice startled Rosemarie. It didn't match the ancient image in the reflection. She turned her head to see from the corner of her eye the woman holding her. She could not be a year older than 28.

"Stop," Rosemarie said, scared and trying to make sense of what had just happened.

The young woman stopped but continued to hold on providing the same support and stability. Rosemarie angled an eye for a clearer side glance. The young woman, taller and inches from her own face, wore nurse's scrubs. She smelled like cigarette smoke. She had dark hair, short and straight. Her skin appeared Mediterranean and was without a blemish. She had crooked slightly yellowed teeth, which diminished a bit from her otherwise striking beauty.

Rosemarie looked from the window reflection back to the young lady and then back again. She noticed one feature was exactly as she remembered it in the reflection—the eyes. They were dark, and they radiated a deep light. Rosemarie, accepted, nodded, steadied in the confident arms, and let the young woman lead her back to bed.

"My name's Trish. I'm your nurse today."

"Trish, when can I leave?"

"That's unusual," Trish said with a smile in her tone. "What's the hurry?"

Rosemarie concentrated on her walking, not sure how to easily explain the situation. When they reached the bed, Trish leaned over and released the bed rail and helped her turn to sit. Slowly she sat.

"Would you like to sit in a chair, go to the bathroom, or lie down for a few moments?"

"What will get me home sooner?"

Trish sat on the bed next to her, covered her hand and squeezed slightly.

"Let me check a few things," she said. "Do you want to lie down or sit?"

Rosemarie thought.

"It is not part of the assessment. There is no wrong answer," said Trish.

"Then, sit me up in bed," said Rosemary.

Trish guided her and electronically maneuvered the bed until she sat up comfortably. She then wheeled over a portable desk with a computer and screen, and with the same graceful precision worked with Rosemarie, the monitoring equipment, and the computer. She glided between tasks with focus and rhythm, one that Rosemarie recognized from years of teaching—she was watching a professional, a young nurse extremely competent in her duties. Her routines and confidence calmed.

"How are you feeling?" said Trish.

"Good." She liked Trish.

Moments passed as Trish typed.

"You really should not smoke. It's bad for you," said Rosemarie.

Trish stopped typing. She looked at Rosemarie, and Rosemarie waited, feeling sorry she had said anything.

"Haaaa!" Trish said in one loud and deep exclamation. "Okay, okay, Miss Heart Attack Know-It-All." Rosemarie could hear the smile in her voice. "Let's get our roles straight. You are the patient. I am the nurse. Clear?"

"Yes," said Rosemarie, liking Trish even more.

"Okay, Miss Bossy, any shortness of breath or other unusual symptoms?"

"I feel sore."

"Where?"

This matter-of-fact questioning continued gently and directly until Rosemarie could feel herself falling asleep. She knew Trish had asked a question but could not remember the question.

"And why do you need to get home today?"

She heard this clearly, rousing her awake and setting off a beeping from one of the monitors.

"Whoa, settle down," said Trish, looking from the monitor to Rosemarie and back.

Rosemarie was not sure how to explain, so she simply said, "My granddaughter."

Trish sat at the edge of the bed and waited.

"My granddaughter is in trouble."

"What kind of trouble?"

"I don't know. Something is hurting her, and I don't know what or what to do about it."

"How old is she?"

"12."

"I think you are describing most 12 year olds," said Trish quietly without a hint of sarcasm. Trish sat not moving or speaking. In their silence, the machines sounded and the wind-swept rain pelted the window.

"This is different. I am losing her, and I do not know what to do. I don't know how to help her."

Trish said nothing. Rosemarie waited. No movement. After a long silence, Trish said, "Do you knit?"

"No."

"Neither do I," said Trish, and she started moving again. She stood up and in fluid, purposeful rhythms took care of work routines, checking the IV lines and monitors and then walking into the attached bathroom.

"This is strange," thought Rosemarie, waiting for more explanation.

"My mother knits," said Trish from inside the bathroom. "And, she also taught high school writing."

"That's nice," said Rosemarie, answering to be polite but feeling misunderstood by Trish's small talk in response to sharing a major problem.

"Did you ever teach?"

"Yes, I taught math," said Rosemarie.

"That'll do," said Trish.

"Do what?"

Trish walked back into the room, opened a cupboard, took something out, closed the cupboard, walked back to the bed, and stood motionless again. The stillness gave weight to the moment.

"Mom used to grade essays during the school year, every night after dinner until bed. She also knit, still does actually," said Trish.

Rosemarie waited for the connection—unable to make one and thinking that trusting this girl, who now seemed a little unbalanced, might have been a mistake.

"She told me solving a problem in life is a lot like untangling balls of yarn or giving guidance to a student who is learning to write."

Rosemarie listened.

"She said the writing of students who were learning resembled the balls of yarn tangled at the bottom of her yarn basket. Looking at the writing problems or the tangled mess of yarn, you did not know where to start to fix the problem—there were too many tangles. Sometimes everything was a mess. It felt overwhelming."

Rosemarie nodded and saw the connection.

"The key my mom would say is to find one thread, just one string of yarn, a thread at the middle of the mess—like for writing she would say—maybe the purpose—and then focus on this one thread. Just untangle and solve the issue for this one thread—and guess what, she would say— most of the other threads seem to untangle themselves."

Rosemarie knew the wisdom before Trish spoke it.

"The key is to do something," said Trish. "Find one thread that seems like an important one and act. Just start untangling. Do not wait for the perfect answer, perfect moment, or perfect time. Just find a thread. There is no perfect."

"Simply pick a thread?" said Rosemarie, articulating aloud her question, which in her mind translated to, "Do I know my granddaughter well enough to know what is the thread?"

Seconds later, the pager hooked on Trish's pocket beeped. She pulled it off, read it, and rushed out of the room, saying, "You'll know. You can find it. I'll be back. Rest now."

Rosemarie heard others rushing down the hall away from her room and heard an intercom announce "code blue" and room number 302. All activity and conversations in the hall outside her room ceased as the action raced away. Her ears tuned back into the timed machinery and the rain pelting and running across the window.

Falling into sleep, she awoke to someone running up the hall coming closer to her door, someone running at that emergency pace toward her room. She looked out the corner of her eye toward the open door to see who would go by. Instead, Madeline burst into the doorway, out of breath and soaked. Rosemarie could feel the storm come in with her. Her hair dripped rain and matted against her face and her clothes smelled drenched through. She dropped something on the floor and stomped her feet and flung her arms to remove the weather, flinging rain in all directions.

"Whoa, whoa! You need a towel," said Rosemarie holding up her hands.

"I'm cold! I forgot my rain coat," said Madeline gasping, "but" she added with pride reaching down for the object next to her, "I remembered to pick up your purse."

"Maddie, get in here and let's get you toweled off. You are going to catch pneumonia!"

She walked forward and held the soaking-wet purse out, each footstep squished with water. "Grandma, I made it. I am here to bring you home," she said with obvious pride.

"There should be a towel in the bathroom. Also, what time is it? Shouldn't you be in school?"

Madeline walked into the bathroom, not answering.

"Does your mother know you are not in school? Does your mother know you are here?"

"Grandma, Mom doesn't know YOU are here!" she countered back.

"Good point."

"I kept your secret," said Madeline coming out of the bathroom with a handful of brown paper towels.

Rosemarie watched her soaking wet and run-ragged granddaughter with a mix of gratitude and guilt. Yes, one lie usually leads to another or one omission to another, and this was not a lesson she planned to teach her granddaughter. Somehow she would have to address this later. For now, she had a more immediate thing to worry about, and it was soaked through in front of her trying to dry off with paper towels.

Rosemarie still had no idea how to help her but at least she had an idea, to find a key thread and just untangle, but first, she had to get her dry and keep her from catching pneumonia.

"Who's tracking puddles in my hall? And, what's the commotion here?" said Trish appearing in the doorway and not sounding amused at all. "Are you trying to ruin my perfect safety record young lady?" she said to Madeline. "That kind of water is a safety hazard, and we are having too many incidents today already." She did not crack a smile and looked from Rosemarie in the bed and back to Madeline in the bathroom doorway and back.

"You need a real towel not a paper towel. Don't move. Stay put."

Madeline stood as directed while Trish exited. Minutes later she returned with a large white towel still warm from a dryer and a hospital gown.

"Get in that bathroom," Trish said with the same matter-of-fact tone she had commanded with previously. "Take off those soaking wet clothes and put on that gown. Where is your raincoat?" she said to Madeline while looking at Rosemarie.

"But," interrupted Madeline almost shouting, "I can't wear a hospital gown. I have come to take my grandma home."

"Child," said Trish, which made Rosemarie smile because Trish was little more than a child herself, "I am not letting you go anywhere soaked through like you are. You'll catch a cold, maybe pneumonia, and based on my day so far, end up in here, which would be just my luck. So, first things first. Get those clothes off now and get in this without argument!"

All in the room heard the commands. Trish had spoken.

Madeline took the gown, went into the bathroom, and closed the door.

"That's my granddaughter," said Rosemarie, beaming.

"I gathered," said Trish using some of the paper towels to dry the floor.

"Everything okay?" asked Rosemarie.

Trish appeared startled by the question. She paused, nodded and said with kindness, "Rosemarie, I am fine. It is a hospital, and there are some very sick people in here today."

"Well, all the more reason for me to go home. I feel great."

"Ha!" laughed Trish, "You have made your case. Let's get you sitting in the chair here. You'll need to demonstrate a few actions like sitting up on your own and going to the bathroom before the doctor will release you, but I'm on your side." Trish began to ready her for moving from the bed to a chair.

Madeline opened the bathroom door with the gown on and tied from the front wrapped completely around twice and covering her securely like an oversized toga. She held the wad of wet clothes in front of her.

"Just lay them on the floor. I'll take them and

ask housekeeping to run them through the dryer." Trish lowered the rail and Rosemarie dropped her feet over the side of the bed, stood, took in a deep breath, and allowed Trish to guide her into the chair. Trish then took the extra blanket folded at the end of the bed and tucked Rosemarie into the chair, saying, "I will bring you both back some world famous hospital soup and tea."

Trish didn't pause, turned to Madeline, and said firmly and kindly, "Now you get in bed here. Get under these covers and get warm. I'll have your clothes back dry in time to get your grandmother home today. We're just waiting for the doctor's visit and sign off."

Madeline did as told. Trish tucked the covers around her, and released the stops on the bed, moving it and lowering it so that Rosemarie's hand could reach her granddaughter's hand. She placed Rosemarie's warm hand on Madeline's cold hand. "I'll be back," Trish said, and scooped up the wet clothes as she left.

For several minutes they sat without word within the rhythms of the rain and hospital monitors.

"You okay?" asked Rosemarie.

"Yes, fine. You okay?"

"Yes."

After a moment of silence, Madeline added, "It's really raining out there."

From the corner of her eye, Rosemarie looked out the window. "Yes, I think winter is here early this year."

"Yep," said Madeline.

On any day before today, Rosemarie would have continued the conversation with safe pleasantries, but in a day everything had changed. She had no idea what the thread could be, and in this thought she turned from the storm to her granddaughter who was firmly tucked up to her neck with the hospital blanket.

"Are you okay?" She asked again.

"Yeah," said Madeline, "I'm fine."

This was obviously not going to reveal the thread. Several moments of awkward silence passed. She felt painfully aware that she really had no idea how to talk to her granddaughter.

"Hon, why don't you take a nap? It'll take a while for your clothes to dry, and you're already in bed."

"What about you?" said Madeline, with a hint of relief.

"It feels good to be sitting up. I feel great. Rest

for a few minutes."

Madeline nodded, rolled to her side, and closed her eyes. Rosemarie felt relieved and wondered if Maddie had complied simply to avoid trying to talk because it was awkward for her too. Whatever the reason, it gave her time to think.

"What is the thread?" thought Rosemarie. She had no idea. This surprised her. The idea that she really did not know her granddaughter well enough to know any answer, anywhere to start, truly surprised her. Until this day, she thought she knew her. Until this day, she knew enough. Now she just did not know. She didn't know at all.

Soon, her granddaughter breathed deeply in sleep, and Rosemarie thought about what she did know. She knew about the world surrounding her. She knew her parents struggled and were not perfect. "God knows," she spoke to herself, "I could have been a better mother to Claire, but there is no time for this pity party now." For all the generational shortcomings, Claire loved Madeline, and like all the generations before, this love could overcome unprepared and preoccupied parenting. She knew Madeline had loved grade school and excelled in reading, art, and math. She was particularly pleased with the math, not only because she had taught math but because fluency in math would be an advantage for her future options. She knew she had friends in grade school, and.... Rosemarie paused. She flashed to a memory a little over 11 years ago when she held her as a baby. Madeline was the most beautiful baby. Images of Madeline appeared in her mind's eye from infancy through grade school.

"That's strange," she thought. Rosemarie could not envision her granddaughter's life in junior high. All the memories and images merged from before junior high. She realized her granddaughter had walked into adolescence, and Rosemarie had let her go and did not know her granddaughter's world anymore.

This was a significant problem now because not knowing enough about her—at this time—she could not identify a thread to grab. She needed to get to know her again. She listened to her sleeping with rhythmic breathing.

"I love you Maddie," she whispered, letting the message linger within the rhythms of breath, and rain, and machines, and she hoped that this love would be enough to guide her.

Chapter 11
Claire's Rage

Furious couldn't begin to describe Claire's rage. Now that the drama had ended, she felt embarrassed and exhausted, and absolutely incensed at her daughter.

Inside her work cubicle, she sat waiting, unable to concentrate, having wasted an entire afternoon of productive work dealing with the Madeline issue. She wished for solid walls and a thick door. Instead, she listened to her colleagues type, answer phones, and pretend to be uninterested.

All of life's trivia and pain seeped through the fabric-covered partitions and provided fodder for gossip and comparison. Claire prided herself in keeping her personal life and the lives of her family confined to her cubicle, and only allowing the seepage of carefully planned personal press releases, which she presented as random, easily overheard conversations. Now—in one day—her private partitions had exploded, and she sat exposed and internally tumbling from waves of furor to receding numbness and shame.

She sighed as the numbness rolled in again. She scanned the piles of paper covering her desk. Each pile in some way supported the draft grant stacked next to the computer keyboard in front of her. Strangely, the piles felt comforting, organized and orderly.

Her work phone rang. She grabbed it quickly before the second ring.

"Hello?" she said trying to keep her voice calm.

"Claire?" asked a man's voice.

"Yes," she replied, relieved in recognizing his voice.

"This is Dr. Hancock returning your call. I am sorry for the delay; it's 4:50 p.m., and this is my first break from patient sessions. I tried your cell phone, but no one answered."

"My cell phone is dead. I left my charger at home," Claire said in one breath, lowering her voice and cupping her hand over her mouth and the phone's receiver.

"Doctor," she continued in the next breath, "I need your help. Can you please move Madeline's appointment to tonight or tomorrow morning? This is an emergency." Under each word, Claire suppressed tears from this first moment of relief in a spent afternoon bouncing from terror to rage.

"What is the problem, Claire?"

"Oh God," she said using all remaining energy to stay mad and hold in her tears. "I need your help."

"What is the problem, Claire?"

"Madeline skipped school this afternoon. She had accessed a non-sanctioned website—a bloody blog about something called QiGong and finding one's inner beauty. I know that man led her to this site!"

"What man?"

"The hippy pervert she's been hanging out with. Oh God, I'm so embarrassed!" Claire whispered.

"Why are you embarrassed?"

"Some teacher's aide found Madeline's

assigned computer with the URL in the browser line. The URL led to this new-age website thingy. As a result, she was called to the principal's office, and this is how they discovered her missing."

"Missing?"

"Yes, I started an Amber Alert for a missing child because I thought she'd gone to him, and he's at least 25, maybe 30. I got the entire office worked up about this." Claire took in and let out a deep breath. Breathing was difficult.

"That seems appropriate considering the situation. They obviously found her," said Dr. Hancock. "Is she okay?"

"I don't know. She called about 30 minutes ago. We called off the Amber Alert not long after I initiated it, but the entire office got involved. This is so embarrassing. I'm so incredibly mad at her."

"Is she okay?" Dr. Hancock repeated.

"I don't know. She's at home with her grandmother. She says she was with her grandmother." Then, Claire paused and added angrily. "That kid is a piece of work. She seemed more concerned about upsetting my mother, her grandmother. She asked me not to share with her that she had been caught skipping school. When did my mother's feelings get into this?!"

Claire paused, took a deep breath, and continued, "She swears she did not see the man, but she will not tell me why she skipped school. Dr. Hancock, I think she's in big trouble. I think she displayed the URL as a cry for help."

Dr. Hancock said nothing, and Claire continued, "I'm so embarrassed. I need your help. I don't know how to reach her, and frankly, right now I could beat her. I've never beaten her, never, but...but I could. I could right now."

"It's probably best for right now," Dr. Hancock interrupted, "if you separate your anger, which is a normal mother's response to such a very frightening event, from your joy that you have found her. Can you do this?"

"Joy?" said Claire.

"Focus on the positive right now from finding her uninjured. There will be time to punish after we know more. Does this make sense?"

"I don't know."

"I think it's important right now that you do not act on your emotions of anger. You need to determine an appropriate punishment, possibly with Madeline's help, after we've gathered more information and we've worked through some of your anger. I doubt escalating will help right now."

"I hear you. What should I do?"

"First, recognize that your feelings matter. You have a right to be angry and embarrassed. These feelings are appropriate."

"Yes, but what do I do?" Claire repeated annoyed at the condescending psychological pep talk.

"You go home; you hug your daughter. You tell her that she scared you to death. You tell her that you love her, and you thank the universe that she is alive and hopefully uninjured," Dr. Hancock said.

In the silence, from the depths of Claire's embarrassment and anger and profound relief, she leaned forward and began to cry.

"Then, and hear me here," continued Dr. Hancock, "You tell her firmly but with control, that her actions hurt you deeply and that she will be punished appropriately, but for now, you can't decide on a punishment because you are too upset and too overjoyed that she is alive and at home. Can you do this?"

Claire swallowed her tears to speak. "Yes," she mumbled.

"Okay, I can see her tomorrow at 8:00 a.m.

You will need to come too. Most likely I will see you for 10 minutes, Madeline for 30, and both of you for another 10. Will this work?"

"Yes, thank you."

"Claire."

"Yes."

"You've been through a lot. Take care of yourself tonight. Don't beat yourself up. You did the right things. Now wait to act until you have more information. You'll need to sit with all your emotions and be patient. Can you do this for me?"

"Yes."

"Okay, I will see you and your daughter tomorrow morning."

Claire hung up the phone, cupped her hands over her face, and sobbed. She knew others could hear her, realized her makeup was running, and felt her face blotching beyond a touchup, and she didn't care, for the first time in any recent memory, she just didn't care.

After several minutes, she heard someone stop and stand behind her at the entrance of her cubicle. She didn't turn around. She lifted her head from her hands.

"What can I do?" asked Vicki's voice from behind her.

"She's home. She's safe," Claire answered, not turning around to see her. "You can do nothing, but thank you for your support today. Thank you very much."

"Let me know if I can help, Claire."

Claire said nothing, until she realized that Vicki had not left, so she added, "Really, thank you. I'll have the draft for the building grant to you tomorrow. We're still on schedule."

A few minutes later, Claire listened to her leave, looked at her computer clock, and felt relieved that it was 5:10 p.m. Most others had gone home; she could walk out alone. She stood for the first time in hours and looked out over the maze of cubicles. She noticed the rain—she could hear it against the darkened windows beyond the cubicles. She paused. She had not noticed the storm all day.

Stuffing the draft copy of the grant into her briefcase along with her purse, she put on her coat and walked toward the window. Too dark to see outside, she watched her reflection become clearer as she approached the window. It reflected back her face, distorted, shadowed, and drawn, moving slightly in and out of focus against the streaks of water and storm, like a rain-soaked Picasso.

Stopping a foot from the reflection, she reached out her hand and touched her face in the window. It felt cold.

Chapter 12
Madeline's Promise

Madeline entered the waiting room behind her mother and sat on a vinyl plump-cushioned chair, which did not sink in with her weight but remained plump and slippery. She reached out to the armrests to balance her body in the chair and slid to one side. The metal frame felt cold. Her mother handed her one of two clipboards with a pen from the coffee table and said, "Each of us needs to fill out this form separately."

She felt relieved to have something to do. During the 20-minute drive to the office, her mother did not speak, not one word. Last night her mother said only three sentences to her, carefully pronouncing each word evenly in a controlled calm that contrasted with the obvious anger visible in her face. "I am busy tonight making up for all the work I missed today because of your extreme irresponsibility. Therefore, I expect you to make dinner for your grandmother and to keep her entertained. If you know what is good for you, you will not interrupt me tonight."

Madeline began filling out her form. "Mom," she asked timidly, "what do I put for insurance information?"

"I'll fill that out on mine," Claire said, not looking up from her form.

Madeline filled in her personal data, and then began circling numbers from 1 to 7 in response to specific statements about her feelings, sleeping, and eating habits. According to the directions, she should circle 7 for "strongly true" statements.

"I often feel inadequate." Madeline read the statement and positioned her pencil over the 7. Yes, she thought, this was strongly true, but just to be on the safe side, she marked the 4. She wished the scale had a neutral, in-the-middle number.

For the next several minutes, she pondered statements, usually deciding that it really depended on the day and the situation, and then she chose the 3 or 4 just to be safe. The 3s and 4s seemed like what normal people might answer for statements like, "Sometimes I feel sad about the world."

The final part of the form asked two questions: Why are you here today? What are your treatment goals? For the first question she wrote, "My mother told me to come." She pondered the second question. Like most of the previous questions, an answer seemed to depend on the moment.

"My treatment goal is for my mother to like me," she thought looking up and over to her mother who seemed confused by one of the questions. Knowing this sounded pathetic and could result in talking longer to this counselor, whom she really didn't want to talk to, she thought about safe statements: "to make my mother happy….to be responsible….to be the person my mother wants me to be….to not have my mother mad at me all the time….to be a better person….to grow up….to be more responsible."

The inner office door opened, and a tall, lean man about her father's age, stepped into the waiting room. He wore pressed jeans and a light blue polo shirt. He had business-cut hair, short and trimmed above the ears. He didn't look like a doctor. He looked more like a grade school teacher who ran a lot and ate vegetables.

"Hello Claire," he said. Then, he looked directly at Madeline and said, "You must be Madeline," with a welcoming and gentle smile. He definitely acted like a grade school teacher.

She nodded.

"Well, welcome. I have met your mother and father before and heard wonderful things about you. I'm glad you could make it today. Let me take those clipboards."

He reached out and took both clipboards and said, "Let me share an approach. If this works for you both, I will spend about 10 minutes talking to your mother alone to hear her concerns, and then I will bring her back here and spend time talking with you, Madeline, and finally I will bring you both in to my office to discuss how we can work together toward some mutually beneficial outcomes. Will this work for both of you?"

"Yes," said Claire, and Madeline nodded.

"Okay, let's get started. Claire come with me. Madeline make yourself at home. We have all variety of magazines. The bathroom is out that door and down the hall to your right. We will be back in 10 minutes and 20 at the latest." The door shut behind them.

Madeline liked his eyes; they seemed kind and a little sad.

After a few moments sitting uncomfortably, she stood and walked slowly around the waiting room, circling the coffee table. Placing the heel of her right foot to the toe of her left, she counted her feet around the table, one, two, three… 12, balancing along an imaginary line. She tried this again walking in a slightly wider circle, wondering how many extra feet this might add. Hum, 14. Picking up *Sports Illustrated*, she reviewed the cover. She picked up *Woman's Day* and flipped through the pages. A few subscription cards fell out. She picked these up and stuffed them back between two pages. She positioned all 10 magazines from two piles into a fanned display, carefully arching and measuring the covers into an exact span. Having run out of obvious distracting activities, she tapped her fingers on the coffee table and began to worry.

She imagined what her mother was telling the counselor. She couldn't imagine the words, but she could feel the anger. She could see her mother sharing this anger, and she imagined the counselor's eyes when he opened the office door, stone cold—black and angry—full of disappointment. She missed her dad.

A few minutes later, she heard steps and her mother's voice. She grabbed a magazine to appear to be reading and did not look up when the door opened.

"Madeline, it's time. Please come with me," he said in the same kind voice.

She stood and looked at her mother. She looked tired but not angry. Standing in the doorway, Dr. Hancock held out his hand motioning for Madeline to join him. He smiled warmly. He turned. She followed, passing by her mother.

They walked down a hallway lined with framed wilderness photography and entered a door at the end of the hall.

"Please sit," he said, pointing to a black leather couch and shutting the door behind them.

She sat upright on the end of the couch, next to the door and farthest away from his chair across from the couch. She angled her body toward him with her hands folded in her lap. Her heart raced.

He placed the clipboard with her data sheet on the table next to his chair, and sat. He watched her for a moment and smiled again.

The room seemed dark. A full-walled shelf filled with books lined the wall across from the couch and behind him. She tried not to look around and waited awkwardly for him to say something.

"Thank you for coming, Madeline," he said gently. "Before we get started, let me explain some of the rules because it is very important for you to know that you can trust me and that I will not lie to you or abuse your trust in anyway. Okay?"

"Yes."

"I believe my role here is twofold." He paused, appearing to think carefully about his words and continued softly as if speaking in a library. "First, we are determining, with your help, if you need my help. Does that sound okay?"

"Yes."

"Second we are helping you and your mother communicate better." He paused and asked, "Would you like this?"

"Yes."

"Good. Now some business before we begin." He raised his voice to a normal speaking tone but kept a slow, comforting pace. "Because you are under 14 years old, I am obligated by the state to share with your mother my written treatment notes if she asks and to share anything you tell me that indicates you may harm yourself." He paused and added more slowly, "I have a good memory. I use the notes for more clinical comments, which is important and essential for insurance, but I need to make this clear. Is this clear?"

"Yes."

"Here's the dilemma: For our sessions to work, you need to know that you can share private information with me that I will not share with your mother, and I need to follow ethical counseling guidelines."

Madeline nodded. His words reminded her of the procedure rules her teachers read each year before handing out the state's standardized tests: "Look only at your own computer. We will hand out one piece of scrap paper. If you must go to the bathroom, raise your hand, and…" But, these test rules were read in a tired monotone, and Dr. Hancock's words were spoken with concern.

"Here's how we can protect your privacy and meet my ethical obligation. You have my word that I will not share with your mother anything you share with me unless I first gain your permission, with one exception," he said holding up one finger.

Madeline watched his long skinny finger.

"If you plan to hurt yourself or another person physically, or if someone else might hurt you emotionally or physically, I will do what is necessary to protect you, which could mean sharing this information. Is this clear? Your safety is a top priority here."

Madeline nodded. She couldn't imagine who might hurt her, besides her mother, or what safety issues he might be talking about and thought about asking for an example, but decided nodding was the right answer, and she nodded again.

"Great," he smiled and clapped his hands. "Let's get started."

The clap announced a new energy in the room, like something big might happen.

"Madeline, do you know why you are here today?" He said picking up the clipboard and turning it over and looking at the bottom of the page to the goals question.

"I am here because my mother is very upset with me."

He nodded without looking up and scanned her answers, turning the pages and guiding his eyes with his skinny finger. He put down the clipboard and looked directly at her. "Do you know why she is upset?"

The question hung in the air for a moment until Madeline filled the silence. "Do you mean overall or this last time?"

Dr. Hancock studied her and smiled. "How about we focus today on this last time?"

"Yes."

"Yes, you know why she is upset?"

"Yes."

"Can you share with me?"

Madeline knew she was simply repeating what he already knew. "I skipped classes yesterday afternoon at school."

"Do you usually do this?"

"No."

"Have you ever done this before?"

"No."

"I imagine then that you had a good reason."

"Yes," Madeline said and her thoughts flashed to the unbelievable adventure of the previous afternoon—to the sprint to the house for the purse, to the sprint to the hospital in the pouring rain, to the joy in seeing her grandmother, to the surprising warmth of the gown and the bed, to unexpected sleep, to delicious soup brought by the nurse "to feed their souls," to the doctor check in, to the checkout, to the taxi ride home. They made it home. She kept her secret. Grandma was okay. She kept the secret.

"Madeline?" he said and brought her thoughts back to the moment. "Can you share the reason you skipped school with me?

Madeline paused and looked at Dr. Hancock. Her heart pounded. She looked down at the couch and tapped the leather. She sat back and then shuffled and leaned forward again. The room temperature felt hot.

"Is it hot in here?"

"I don't think so," he responded and waited.

She hadn't preplanned describing what she had been doing. She needed to protect her grandmother's secret. Quickly she thought about his rule. What was the exact wording related to being hurt?

She looked at him. He sat back in his chair. He looked patient, like he had hours to wait for an answer. The possibility of Grandma entering a nursing home is hurting someone. She had a heart attack that might have killed her. She had heart surgery that might have killed her. She could be put in a nursing home and that might kill her. All these facts and possibilities involve someone potentially being hurt. She thought about asking for a clarification about the secrecy rule—if it just involved her being hurt or another family member being hurt.

"Are you okay?" he asked leaning forward.

Madeline flinched. She couldn't risk telling him; he might be forced to tell her mother, and she had to keep her grandmother's secret. She had to keep her grandmother out of a nursing home.

"Yes," she answered, stalling.

"What can you tell me?"

"I was helping someone."

"You were helping someone?" he asked.

"Yes."

"I see. Can you tell me about that?"

"No, I promised not to tell," Madeline said immediately dreading her words as they came out. She wished she could think of a lie, but she couldn't think fast enough to lie. She had never been a good liar. In fact, from her experience, as was confirmed again yesterday, whenever she did anything the least bit sneaky or close to a lie, she got caught.

"You promised not to tell," he repeated.

"Yes," she whispered feeling the weight of her promise.

"Well, this is a dilemma," he said reflectively sitting back in his chair.

At least two minutes passed. He said nothing and Madeline waited. She liked him. He seemed kind. He was trying. She could tell he wanted to help. Sadly, she knew that probably he would get mad at her too and be disappointed in her just like her mother, but she promised not to tell, and she needed to protect her grandmother. She promised.

"Have you heard about good secrets and bad secrets, Madeline?"

"Yes," Madeline felt embarrassed. She remembered in third grade a school counselor coming to her class and discussing "good" secrets. Examples the school counselor gave were when she liked a boy and decided to wait to tell him or sent him a valentine and didn't tell him. "Bad" secrets involved things like when adults asked children to do things with them and to not tell anyone, especially if these things made you feel uncomfortable.

Madeline knew her grandmother's secret fit the definition of a bad secret but that it was not a bad secret, but she couldn't explain why. At this point, she figured yes and no answers might be the best approach. She simply needed to do what was necessary to get through this counseling session.

"Are you keeping a bad secret, Madeline?" Dr. Hancock asked.

Madeline looked at him and looked away. She wanted to leave.

"You've done nothing wrong."

Madeline looked at him. She wasn't sure what he meant. She had skipped school and been caught. That was wrong.

"I know you like this person, and I know you are trying to protect this person," he said softly, "but adults do not ask children to keep secrets."

Madeline nodded. She agreed in principle.

He repeated, "You have done nothing wrong."

She nodded.

"Has this person hurt you?"

"No."

"Has he asked you to do things you feel embarrassed about or do not want to do?" he asked softly with gentleness.

Madeline paused. Dr. Hancock had said "he," but she knew he had no way of knowing about the person's gender. She wanted to correct him, but she felt the least she said the better.

"No," she said.

"Has he touched you inappropriately?"

"No." The questions were getting strange.

"Are you sure?" he asked in a strong and concerned tone.

"I am sure," she replied firmly.

"You know, I had a patient once, a young sensitive woman like yourself, I think she was even your age, and she cared deeply for an adult who said he loved her. She needed to be loved. She felt lonely. Do you feel lonely?"

Madeline said nothing. She could relate to the girl he knew.

"Do you feel lonely sometimes?" he said leaning forward and cupping his hands together.

"Yes."

"Doesn't it feel wonderful to have someone in our lives that needs us? I bet your friend needs you. Is that right?"

Madeline thought about her grandmother. "Yes," she answered.

"That must make you feel pretty special."

Madeline nodded, not quite sure what to say.

"Does he play the guitar?" he asked softly.

The question stumped Madeline. She wasn't sure if grandmother played the guitar. She knew she played the piano. If she played the piano, she might know how to play the guitar.

"I guess so."

"Does he play for you?"

"No."

"What do you do together?" he asked nonchalantly.

Madeline saw the trap and paused. She raced through what she had done with her grandmother lately: called 911, did CPR, took the ambulance ride with her, helped check her into a hospital, released her from the hospital, and discussed God and prayer while waiting for the release and taking the taxi home. Only one of these she could discuss honestly and openly.

"We discuss God and prayer."

"You discuss God and prayer?" he said with his look of concern immediately changing to a look of confusion.

"Yes."

"Why?" he asked, still looking confused, but as if noticing and correcting his own facial expression, smiled gently again.

"I guess because it is important. Do you believe in God?" she asked.

"Do I believe in God?" he replied, looking confused again.

"Yes. Do you believe in God?" repeated Madeline.

"Well, that is a big question," he said, leaning back in his chair, frowning in thought, and staring back at her, waiting, as if he were deciding something important in the wait.

He sighed, smiled carefully, sighed again, nodded, as if saying yes, and asked: "Have you heard of Carl Jung?"

"I think so."

"He's one of the founders of modern psychology. He was a brilliant man. I admire him tremendously. Anyway, he talks about a universal force."

Madeline nodded.

"I believe in his universal positive force. I am not sure if this force takes the form of a man, a woman, a child—or God. I do believe each of us has this force inside us. That is probably as close to believing in a conventional God that I can come. Do you believe in God?"

Madeline thought about the question. No one had asked her before. "My," she paused almost saying grandmother and stopped herself inserting "friend."

"My friend believes deeply in God and prays to God every day. Do you believe in prayer?"

Dr. Hancock nodded his head yes. "I do believe that the universal force can help us each and every day, because I witness it in my practice." He paused, appeared to be thinking about something, and added, "Sometimes people forget to ask for the help they need. Do you need help, Madeline?"

Madeline thought about the question. She needed so much. God must get overwhelmed with the requests of people. She started thinking about all she needed. She needed her mother to stop hating her. She needed to keep her grandmother out of a nursing home. She needed her father home. She needed to fit into junior high. She needed friends. She needed to succeed in school so that she could get into a good college. She needed to be smarter. She needed to study more. She needed to like math again. She needed to be a different person who people liked, who was popular. She needed…Madeline raced through the needs until Dr. Hancock interrupted.

"Can I help you, Madeline?"

"I'm looking for my prayer," Madeline blurted out.

"Looking for your prayer?"

"Yes, I think God must feel completely tired and overwhelmed by all of our needs. He must get billions of prayers a day."

"I don't think you are limited to one prayer," said Dr. Hancock.

"Maybe not, but if God listens to our prayers, all the billions of requests, then I think it is pretty important to have one clear request and not confuse God with lots of little things."

"So, what is your one prayer for God?"

"I don't know yet; I'm still thinking about it. I'm still looking," Madeline said, feeling the frustration in her voice as she spoke.

Dr. Hancock nodded but said nothing, just watched her carefully as if trying to determine something.

"What?" she asked.

"I think my historical mentor Carl Jung might say that your life is the answer."

"What?"

"The answer to your one prayer," he paused and nodded, "It is your life, Madeline." He looked at her for a long moment and added, "and the important thing is to keep looking. This is healthy. Good."

"What?" Madeline said again, not really understanding what he meant.

"Keep looking and tell me what you find," he said, seeming genuinely interested.

He then clapped his hands again, looked for his clipboard, picked it up, and said, "Madeline," in a more business-like tone, "Do you plan to skip school again?"

"Nooo," she said, wondering where the conversation was going now.

"Do you plan to do anything illegal in the next week?"

"Noooo," she said carefully, still wondering how the conversation took on this new direction.

"Do you plan to do anything dangerous or anything that might harm you?"

"No," she said.

"We're running out of time today," he said glancing through her answers again and then looking up. "In a minute I want to bring your mother back into the room. If this works for you, when your mother returns, I'd like to make a plan for the week."

"A plan for the week?"

"Your mother is worried about you. I'd like to see both of you separately next week and into the near future until we can arrive at a place where you can both feel validated and can communicate more positively as you transition through adolescence."

Madeline nodded.

"In a plan, we all agree to interact, to communicate and act, in agreed upon ways until we can learn to communicate and interact more naturally, which we will work to do in the next few months," he said.

Madeline nodded, listening carefully. He might be able to help her with her mother.

"For example, when your mother comes in, I will schedule separate appointments for you next week, and I will ask her what she needs from you until these appointments. Then, I will ask you what you need from her."

Madeline thought she knew what he meant, but she wasn't exactly sure.

He continued, "For example, your mother may say that she needs you to attend school each day, come home from school each day at a specific time, and not spend time with anyone except family and your school friends."

He paused and Madeline could tell he was reading her to see how she might react to his examples. These examples seemed fair. She said nothing.

"Can you do these things if she asks? Can you especially only see the people outside of school she asks you to see for one week?"

The request seemed strange, but she felt she could do this. "Yes, I think so."

"Madeline," he said firmly, "Until we can get this sorted out, I need you to commit that you will not see anyone outside your family or school that your mother does not know. Is this something you can do for a week until we see each other again? I need truth here."

"Okay," she said, not understanding why this would be difficult at all, but he seemed to think it was a major issue. He waited, again saying nothing, so she added to stop the uneasiness, "Yes, I can agree to only spend time with family and friends that my mother knows." This all seemed very strange, but she needed to get the session over with and get back home.

He continued. "Now, on your end, for what your mother needs to do for you, you may say that you need your mother to spend time with you at dinner or help you with your homework. Only you really know what you need from your mother, but this is a good time to think about this. The expectations are for both of you. This is a key to quality communication and building family bonds."

Madeline began thinking about what she could ask from her mother. She knew her one impossible request: don't hate me so much. However, this sounded like a pathetic need, one that if spoken could embarrass her mother. Madeline knew all the things her mother did for her (because she reminded her recently)—she worked, paid the mortgage, bought the food, cooked the food, purchased her clothes.... She did all of these things. As she was constantly re-minded, she did what a mother was supposed to do. Another kid might be grateful, but she needed what her mother could not seem to give.

"Madeline," he asked, "Are you okay with this plan?"

"Sure," she said, in a voice that to her sounded far away. "Bring Mom back in. I'm ready."

Chapter 13
Rosemarie's Challenge

"Hi, how was school?" asked Rosemarie.

"Good," said Madeline.

"Did you do anything fun?"

"Not really."

"Are you learning anything interesting?"

"Not really."

"I see. What is your favorite subject?"

"I guess that depends."

Since returning from the hospital, Rosemarie endured variations of this conversation each afternoon when Madeline returned from school. She could tell that her granddaughter was not hiding anything or avoiding conversation; she simply had nothing she felt was interesting to share. Even knowing this, Rosemarie felt inadequate.

"How can I find the thread when I can't even have a meaningful conversation with this child?" she asked God each night as she sat before her Bible at the little desk in the study/guest room. No answer appeared. In the silent response, she knew intuitively she simply had to keep praying, trying to connect, and staying open for any thread.

As days passed into weeks, she settled into the same pattern. She got up when she heard Claire's alarm go off, went to the kitchen, made coffee for her and her daughter, and using all her energy to appear awake and energetic, drank her coffee as her daughter and granddaughter swirled around her and hurried off to work and school.

Each day after they left the house, she settled back into bed exhausted and slept for several more hours until 10:00. Her body still ached from the surgery, and she felt surprised at how the anesthetic seemed to still linger in her body and ooze out slowly. Each day she felt slightly more energy and slightly less internally bruised. Some days, and these were difficult days, she had follow-up appointments at the hospital, and she had to carefully plan to get there and back with no one noticing and still have energy for her primary task—finding the thread. On her first outing, she set up a post office box at a neighborhood postal annex for the delivery of all mail related to her hospital stay and follow-up doctor's appointments.

No matter what the daily duty and chore, she was prepared and ready for Madeline when she came home from school "to watch her grand-mother." Yes, she knew she was an assigned chore, although Madeline had not told her and never indicated that she was anything less than interested in spending time with her, Rosemarie knew. She just knew. And, this intuition was confirmed when she overheard Claire telling John in one of their phone conversations that "she is taking her punishment well, and does not seem too upset about having to watch her grandmother after school."

Rosemarie did not laugh then; it stung, but she laughed now—she was "a punishment," an official punishment. "Whatever," she thought, hearing the word her granddaughter said to Claire when they argued. Rosemarie felt blessed that her granddaughter was forced to be with her. Without this forced time and confinement, she had no idea how she could find the thread that might help her. And, frankly, speaking with her granddaughter often felt uncomfortable enough that she would have been inclined to leave her alone in her bedroom or in front of the TV. But, as she thought and smiled, "if I am going to be a punishment, I guess I might as well be a memorable one."

And even though she smiled at the thought, she felt inadequate and inept each day as she tried to connect. She thought she knew Madeline, and she knew she had once. She had known Madeline the baby—the crying, laughing, cuddly baby, whose smile became the world each time they would visit. And, she had known Madeline the grade school girl. This was the one who showed such kindness and consideration to her family and school friends, and who when she visited would share about class trips, about children's books, about movies, about her favorite subject—math, and on and on and on. She shared and shared. Rosemarie could see intuitively, she could feel, that Madeline was still Madeline somewhere inside, but she had no idea how to connect to this energetic child she remembered, and she could not understand how to connect to the young adult she had become. Ironically, 30 years of high school teaching had not prepared her for this challenge. That was easy. For this, she prayed and reached out each day trying, but she had no idea what she was doing or if it was working, and it took all her energy.

In the absence of conversation and in the lack of any leads, Rosemarie decided to fill their time together with a useful skill. They would use their time together from 3:30 to 6:00 to plan, shop, and make dinner. It gave them something useful to do together.

Initially, Rosemarie based the meals on her standards—spaghetti, chicken casserole, vegetarian pizza—but soon they planned together, considering family preferences and budget. On Fridays, they sat at the kitchen table with the family laptop and searched the internet for recipes that matched the key ingredients they found listed on sale at the local grocery store. One week, the sale items might include mushrooms, chicken, and peppers. Therefore, they planned for multiple meals using these key ingredients, and as Rosemarie demonstrated, froze or freeze dried the extras to be main ingredients for future weeks. By Friday at dinner (which involved reheating and was dubbed the "leftover" meal), they had their grocery list for the following week, which Claire used to purchase the next week's groceries.

Rosemarie hoped she was teaching her granddaughter how to plan, budget, use a few ingredients for several meals, and not waste. What they cooked and how it tasted did not matter as much to her. It usually tasted just fine, fresh and flavorful. Because Madeline didn't share her stories with any detail, Rosemarie filled their cooking time with stories about her mother and grandmother, and about the stories that define a family.

So it was that one day, when all the ingredients were fresh and the expensive protein on a half-price sale, Rosemarie shared another family story during the meal's preparation, and after the silence, the reflection in all stories heard, Madeline gave her back a thread.

"Now, that the shell is off, let me show you how to de-vein that shrimp," said Rosemarie, cradling the medium-sized prawn in one hand, tilting her head to see the black stripe from the corner of her eye, and surgically slitting it with a sharp paring knife in the other hand, more based on feel than sight, but hitting her mark and pulling up and out the vein.

"My eyesight is not what it used to be. The knife is very sharp, so you need to be delicate and patient. This is not a fast or chop step or you will butcher the shrimp, or worse, your hand. Understood?"

"Yes."

"Okay you try." Rosemarie handed over the knife, handle up, and she moved to the cutting board to peel and mince the garlic, a safer task for the seeing-impaired. With these more time-intensive tasks in motion, she began a story, not knowing if Madeline retained them or cared, but after weeks of stories and re-stories and clarifying stories, she really enjoying the telling, with an anticipation and drama she could not have imagined.

"Maddie, I thought of something yesterday, a point to add to the tale about Aunt Ida," began Rosemarie, hearing her own 'this is going to be a long tale so settle in' warning. "These are not stories based on genetics or DNA. They are based on family, and every family has a culture of positive traits that it can pass on—just leave behind the negative ones. My point, it does not matter if you are an adopted child or a child born to the family. The stories are about our family's culture."

"Was I adopted?" said Madeline in a tone that indicated she knew she was not.

"No, and that is not my point."

"What is your point?"

Rosemarie heard the joking in her grand-daughter's voice, and it soothed her.

"My point is that you mentioned an adopted friend at school. Well, her family stories still apply to her because her family searched for her and brought her into the fold."

Familiar silence followed this statement. Rosemarie minced and Madeline de-veined, and Rosemarie relaxed in the moment. She wondered if it were time, but the words came out before she could take them back.

"You know your mother almost had to adopt a child. She and your father wanted you badly. They tried to get pregnant, and it was not happening. They saw several specialists, and just as they were deciding to adopt, you were conceived."

"Really?"

"Yes."

Silence again and motion stopped. Rosemarie waited for more words, and then continued mincing.

"So my birth was not easy?"

"The birth itself—I attended the event with your father you know (we took shifts)—now it was beautiful, and I do not think it was any harder than any other birth—8 hours of labor is not un-usual. All births are excruciating, well maybe not all, but all of mine, but thankfully we forget."

"I mean, Mom had to work to have me?"

"I know your mom, and she has never worked harder for anything, ever, and I never saw her happier about anything."

They de-veined and minced in silence—a long, comfortable silence.

"How was school today?" Rosemarie asked the question, already knowing the answer—okay—but she asked anyway, all part of the daily routine.

"I think I'm flunking math."

The sentence, although almost whispered and spoken without emotion, screamed through the silence. Rosemarie's brain flooded, shocked by the statement and worried about closing the opening. She settled on the least intrusive response with no time to think through options.

"You have always been good at math," she

said careful not to raise her voice or show concern, just to accept the statement.

"I was in grade school. I'm not now."

"Why the change?" Rosemarie had finished mincing, in fact the garlic was now a pile of wet mush, so she reached for more garlic and started the task again.

"I don't know. I guess I'm not very smart."

That statement sent a blaze of anger through Rosemarie, but she focused on the garlic and on breathing.

"I think you are pretty smart," she said matter-of-factly, "In fact, I taught math for 30 years, and I think you are very smart."

"You're my grandmother."

"Well, that's true," said Rosemarie, internally panicking because the opening was slipping away. "Hon, can you share a few more details? Explain what is happening?"

"Well," she said with a sigh, "I have these computer packets that I work on each day."

"You don't have a teacher?" she questioned, very careful to sound matter-of-fact as her heart beat loudly in her ears.

"Yes, but he sits at the desk and reads. He will come over and help if you raise your hand, but I don't have any questions for him."

"Hmm," said Rosemarie, processing the information and about to ask a question when Madeline added,

"I wish I could be in the smart kids' class. They solve math problems together, and sometimes—I see them when I go by their class on my way to the restroom. They solve real problems, like the forces that our neighborhood bridge needs to function. I heard them talking about this. In our class no one talks. We just spend all day working through these packets, and if we finish enough we get a good grade. I'm having a hard time focusing. It's not very interesting anymore."

"It isn't?" said Rosemarie, feeling an anger from the deepest reaches of her being that she had not felt since Claire had been bullied as a child. "Really, self-study packets with a teacher who reads to himself in class. Hmm. I see, and why with your exceptional math background were you not selected for the 'smart kid class?'" said Rosemarie, hearing her own sarcasm and catching herself.

Madeline must have heard it too because she stopped talking. The silence now was awkward and filled with tension.

"Grandma, are you mad at me?" Madeline finally asked sounding tired and scared.

"No honey!" Rosemarie answered immediately. "Put that knife down." She put her own knife down, wiped her hands, and put her hands on her granddaughter's shoulders. "Look at me," she said, although she could not see her granddaughter clearly, but she could feel her young spirit, that fragile spirit.

"You are not stupid. You are talented at math. You once loved math, and yes I am mad, but not at you. Do you hear me?"

"Yes," she said in a tone indicating she was still scared by this never-seen emotion from her grandmother.

"Good. I will take care of this."

"Grandma," Madeline interrupted, still sounding scared, "there's nothing to take care of. It's my fault!"

"Maybe it is. Maybe it's not."

"Why are you so mad?" Madeline said, upset now too.

"You must hear me, sweetheart. I am not mad at you. Not at all."

"Then what?"

"I am mad because I understand things about

you, about the system—I guess about limitations of systems—and about life. I understand the consequences of things that you do not understand yet. You will understand someday."

"Like what do you understand that I don't?"

"Like you are smart."

"Grandma," said Madeline, obviously uncomfortable.

"No, stop Maddie. I've had enough. Don't worry, I will handle this."

"What is there to handle?" she pleaded.

"Everything will be okay, but there is one story I have not shared yet."

"What's that?"

"Well, I can share the ending, or maybe it is the beginning, but you will not understand until you are a mother or a grandmother or an auntie."

"What?" Madeline said.

Rosemarie watched her granddaughter.

"What is it?" Madeline said again.

Rosemarie knew she had found the thread, but she was too angry at the moment to care. All she could do was explain with words that would make no sense, and then calm down, get the afternoon back on track, and plan. So, she said the words she knew Madeline could not understand, and she said them with such conviction, they even scared her.

"When the mouse roars, the lion jumps."

Chapter 14
Madeline's Path

In the 15 minutes remaining in class before lunch, Mrs. Colby reminded the students that they had until 6:00 p.m. to email their draft reports, and then she announced a "free write" topic. Other students groaned, to which she predictably and light-heartedly replied, "No, I will not now nor ever let you leave early for lunch. I will squeeze every opportunity for learning from the moment!"

Madeline mouthed the last words with her teacher. She knew the refrain well, and unlike some of her peers, she enjoyed the topic-focused time to write in her online class journal.

"Okay, open your thought journals. We

become better thinkers by writing and better writers by thinking," said Mrs. Colby, and Madeline mouthed this last sentence smiling as she opened her journal, silently reciting the all familiar and comforting words. When she glanced up ready and waiting for the topic, Mrs. Colby smiled back at her, having seen the imitation.

"The topic today again relates to critical thinking and data gathering. If another student tells you something about me or let's say another person, how do you know, from your own experience to date, if this piece of data is accurate without researching it? In other words, how do we personally sift through all the information barraging us and without looking up the facts of each piece of data determine what is true? Okay, you have about 10 minutes to write, and do not 'let the perfect destroy the good.' I simply want your imperfect thoughts documented."

Madeline began to type, and based on many of these 10-minute exercises knew not to edit her thoughts but to simply write them down:

People do the same things if we watch them over time. For example, when my mom gets mad, she yells, and it is best to leave her alone and go do homework. Because of this, I know she has a temper. Her actions tell me she has a temper. I guess it is the actions. Now my grandmother, I have never seen her mad.

Madeline stopped on the word "mad," reread the sentence, and edited it to read, "Now my grandmother, I have only seen her mad once." Her hands hovered over the keyboard, suspended in that thought that in all their afternoons and evening spent together she had only seen her really angry once. She typed the words, "When the mouse roars, the lion jumps!" Somehow she knew that Grandma must think she is a mouse, but why, and who is the lion? None of it made any sense.

Forgetting the assignment, she thought of her grandma who loved to share stories. She shared them when they planned the dinners, shared them when they walked for groceries, shared them when they cooked the dinners, and shared them when they cleaned up the mess. Madeline did not mind hearing them told over and over until she could recite them herself. They felt comforting, something known and something connected, although it seemed strange to be connected to dead people from her past, like they really were not dead but living through the stories and

influencing her now in the lessons they had
learned. Strangely, she felt like she carried them
with her now, not as burdens, but as lights on a
path, guides from past lives, and comfort from the
knowledge of their losses and successes.

In her thoughts, Madeline heard her grandmother's voice—clearly heard the saying, the
words she spoke before introducing stories about
her own grandmother traveling across the Mid-
west to the west in a covered wagon drawn by
horses; before telling about relatives who had
farmed in Kansas during the Great Depression,
surviving years and years of useless land
drowning in waves and waves of dust; before
telling about the first college-educated female in
the family, who funded her college education
working the night-shift in a fish-packing factory
and working weekends as a waitress; before
telling about the grief that defined families with a
child who died and the joy that defined families
with children who thrived; before telling of their
dreams, sorrows, contributions, and prayers,
Grandma said:

"My mother used to say that there are few
mysteries in retrospect." Then, Grandma would
add some version of these words, "But there is no

sense in walking backwards, so walk with confidence the path before you." And, then she would start another story, "Have I told you about Aunt Ida and the great flooded train trip?"

Depending on Madeline's mood, she would either answer yes or no (because she had heard versions of most stories at least once now), and with either answer, Grandma would launch into the tale, and Madeline would listen while chopping vegetables, setting the table, or whisking together the ingredients of a family recipe that Grandma knew by heart.

The class bell rang. Madeline saved her journal, turned off the computer, and darted for the door.

"Stop," Mrs. Colby yelled above the burst of noise in the race to lunch.

Madeline stopped, smiled at this teacher she admired, and waited patiently for the familiar goodbye.

"Do not forget to turn in your assignment to me if you already have not, and have a great rest of your day."

Madeline turned back to the door and waited for others to exit. After a half dozen of her peers jammed through the door in twos or threes, John, the smart and respectful boy who sat in front of her, motioned for her to cut in front of him into the orderly line that now formed.

"Thanks," she said, meeting his eyes and smiling.

"You going to lunch?" he said from behind her.

"Yep, I'm meeting Katie. I think you know her. We do a SMART reading program on Saturdays for grade schoolers."

"Yeah, maybe I can sit with you."

"Sure, we usually meet near the south door," said Madeline, glad that she had said this before they exited the room and fell into the mob of students, most of whom were converging toward the lockers in the path to the lunch room. Madeline knew better than to try to walk side by side with anyone while navigating the flow of the mob because enough students walked against the mob current that it was never a clear path without obstacles.

Sure enough, almost immediately she faced the large frame of a football player (which she knew from the football patch on his jacket). She stopped in front of him, boxed in on both sides by other students, and said as politely as she could, "excuse me." He moved over, letting her pass. A moment later, a small, shy boy grazed her side as he ran past her and others, saying as he bounced from one obstacle to the next, "excuse me, excuse me."

Madeline smiled. She could remember her own panic to get out of that crowd as quickly as the boy. But now, several months later, she had learned to walk her own path at her own pace and try to neither be invisible nor an obstacle. "Just be who you are; it is all we can be," she heard her grandma's words in her head, above the noise of the mob.

As she weaved toward the lockers and lunch, she passed Sarah, a friend on her right, and reached out and waved, warmed at her returned smile. She then spotted Chelsea. She weaved over and tapped on her shoulder. She turned.

"Hi Maddie!"

"Hi, Katie and I, and possibly John, are having lunch. Can you join us?" Madeline shouted.

"Not today," Chelsea shouted back. "We have drama practice at lunchtime now that the play is closer, like a week away. You are going, right?"

"Yeah, my grandma and I are coming."

"Great. I hope you can be in the next play."

"I think I can," Madeline shouted confidently before their locker locations parted them naturally. She waved at Chelsea, and turned toward her locker. She smiled. It was the same scene each day. Today three, and some days as many as five, popular boys blocked her locker as they waited for some attention from Pam, the beautiful girl with the locker next to hers. Actually, she really did not know what made Pam beautiful to boys, and sometimes she tried to break down the ingredients—the hair, the laughter, the perfectly straight and white teeth, the expensive clothes. She really didn't know, but she liked Pam. They said very little, but had formed a mutual respect of sorts.

Madeline walked toward her locker. Grandma said her Aunt Ida acted "like she owned the place but with grace" during challenging times. She paused before the boys and said, "Excuse me, guys. That's my locker." And like all the days before, they parted a path for her, Pam said hi, she smiled back, opened her locker, put in her note-book, took out her lunch, and suppressed the urge to say a line from one of Grandma's stories, "as you were."

Within minutes, she was walking into the

lunchroom, excited to talk with Katie and hopefully see John.

Chapter 15
Rosemarie's Gift

The next morning Rosemarie acted.

After Claire left for work and Madeline for school, she called the school at 8:03 a.m., spoke to the principal's secretary, and asked for an appointment that day to discuss "a very important matter." At 10:40, 20 minutes before the appointment, Rosemarie arrived by bus at the stop across from the main school entrance. She stepped into a light drizzle and hurried across the street, not bothering to put on the rain jacket's hood.

By 10:45 inside the school, she found the administrative offices within a glass wall, and stood at the long counter until a woman's voice

from somewhere inside the room of desks, compu-
ters, and filing cabinets asked, "May I help you?"

"Yes, I am here for my 11:00 appointment with
Dr. Smith."

"Yes, and you are Madeline's….?" said the
woman waiting for Rosemarie to fill in the blank.

"I am her grandmother."

"Oh, I see," said the voice. "Please have a seat,
and Dr. Smith will be out to meet you soon."

A row of chairs lined the glass wall behind
her. Rosemarie asked, "Can you direct me to the
bathroom?"

"Yes," said the voice, "We have an adults-only
bathroom down the hall. Go out the door here,
turn right, and at the first door on your right,
you'll find the bathroom."

She walked out into the silent hall, her shoes
tapping on the vinyl floor. The locker-room smell
of the building, the sound of a teacher lecturing in
a classroom, the dark hall—all of these flooded her
senses and reminded her of teaching. She took in a
deep breath. She loved teaching. She passed the
bathroom and walked farther into the school,
listening to the life from within the classrooms.

The bell rang and startled her off balance.
Within seconds, the noise of adolescent energy

blasted from classrooms as students streamed into the hall. Rosemarie braced herself standing still against a wave of students and let the flood pass. They came from all directions. Although blurry as forms in front of her, she could see them pass near to her side and feel the force of their energy.

No time for the bathroom now, Rosemarie needed to return to the office for her appointment. She turned back using the wall to guide her. Every few seconds, a child would appear in front of her, sometimes saying "excuse me," sometimes stepping out of the way, and sometimes waiting for her to move around, which resulted in an awkward stalemate until the child moved around her because she claimed the wall. Finally, she arrived in the office and sat. Her heart beat unsteadily. Her mouth felt dry. Her ears rang. She waited.

"Hello, I am the Principal, Beth Smith," an authoritative woman's voice said. The woman stood tall and broad with defined short grey hair. As Rosemarie stood and extended her hand to greet her, she knew from her presence and the firm handshake that few students would mess with this woman.

"Please call me Rosemarie."

Rosemarie followed her back to her office. Principal Smith walked to the chair behind her large desk and sat.

"Please have a seat, and if you would like, you can shut the door first."

Rosemarie shut the door.

"How can I help you today, Rosemarie?"

"Are you aware my granddaughter is Madeline?"

"Yes."

"And are you aware that she is gifted in math?"

"No, I was not."

"Well, she is, and she is bored in her current math class. I would like you to move her to the TAG class, the talented class."

"I see," said Dr. Smith, who took a key from her desk, stood, and opened the lock to one of three filing cabinets behind her. She pulled open the cabinet and pulled out a folder. She sat back down, opened it, typed information from the file into her computer, and reviewed the screen clicking on a computer key. She said nothing for several minutes.

Finally she spoke. "According to Madeline's data, she scored highly gifted in math in 1st through 3rd grade. Her fourth and fifth grade scores are above average, but her sixth grade test scores are just average. I think she has been placed in the appropriate class based on these last scores," said Principal Smith.

Rosemarie said nothing. She waited.

"You do know that most parents," and here Dr. Smith paused and added "and grandparents, yes, most relatives would like to see their child in the talented and gifted classes, but we do not have room for everyone, and we need to ensure the child is correctly placed to ensure that the child will succeed. I want your granddaughter to succeed."

Rosemarie waited. She needed to choose her words carefully. "Dr. Smith, you and I both know education. I taught high school math for 30 years, and you and I know why this child's scores went down when they did."

"Well, I am not sure I..."

Rosemarie held up her hand, and calmly and carefully said, "Please, let me continue. You and I both know what it means for her future opportunities if she tunes out of math now, at this age, and we also know she has talent."

"I have many students with undiscovered

talents, and we do the very best we can. However, we need to rely on the test scores because we have very limited resources, and we must ensure children are properly placed to use our resources in the most effective manner."

Rosemarie recognized the bureaucratic speak and understood the principal's message, and in theory she might agree; in the global, detached numbers that she loved, she might agree, but not with this one significant number to her.

"If both the TAG class and the regular class were being taught by the same caliber of teacher in the same creative way, I would not be here, but it is my understanding that one is taught by a talented teacher in an interactive way and the other is taught by an online packet system," Rosemarie said, carefully keeping her voice measured and pleasant.

"Let me state again, we have limited resources and students with all ability levels. The packet system meets the needs of most students. Research shows it works."

Rosemarie realized she was losing, and she could not lose. She tried to smile. Dr. Smith continued to expound on the research related to online math education, but Rosemarie did not hear. Her mind raced. Over the din of the principal's words, she spoke an internal prayer, "God, I have been given this thread, and I am afraid I blew it. How can I help Madeline here? How can this lady hear me?" A thought, an obvious, simple thought came.

"Excuse me," said Rosemarie in a quiet tone, so quiet the principal stopped talking. "I have an idea."

They both waited. An antique classroom clock on the wall ticked loudly.

"Dr. Smith, please allow me to work with Madeline every night on her math homework to keep up with the students in the TAG class. As I mentioned, I was a high school math teacher for over 30 years, and I can help her. If you move her into the TAG class, we can do a one-month trial. If at the end of one month, she is not keeping up, she can return to the packets. Can you please, for a grandmother, do this?"

Dr. Smith sighed. She then typed something into the computer and stared at the screen. "You know," she said sounding tired and sad, "I can't change my curriculum for every parent, or grandparent, who thinks their child is special."

"Please. I am not saying she is special. I am

saying she is my granddaughter, and I can do this for her. I can help, and I want to help. Let me help her, please."

"Well," Dr. Smith sighed.

They both sat silently. The clock ticked.

"You have my word."

"Okay," Dr. Smith said softly in a barely audible tone, and then said sternly and louder, asserting her Principal authority, "I will talk with Madeline today. I will move her to the TAG math class tomorrow, BUT she needs to earn an A on her first test, and her next and next, to prove she can do the work. Know, if she does not excel and excel quickly, I will move her back."

Rosemarie tried to speak, and this time Dr. Smith held up her hand, "Let me speak. And, one more thing, word of this unusual arrangement better never get out from you or your grand-daughter or... I'm not sure what, but it won't be good. Is that understood?"

"Thank you. I understand completely, and you have my word. Thank you."

"Don't thank me—show me."

Dr. Smith walked Rosemarie to the door and surprisingly, she continued walking with her to the main building door. Rosemarie did not know what to say, and the principal said nothing.

Rosemarie opened the door. "It's still drizzling," she said trying to fill the silence. Dr. Smith said nothing.

"Thank you," Rosemarie added.

"I have a granddaughter," said Dr. Smith quietly, and she turned. Rosemarie stood in the open door, and listened to her walk away, her heels clicking on the floor, steady and rhythmic, like the ticking of the seconds of an antique clock.

Chapter 16
Claire's Gift

Claire inched her sedan forward, gaining a few feet in the long line of traffic and stopped again. Delayed by a budget meeting, she started home 20 minutes late, merging directly into the evening rush hour. Now stuck in the early winter darkness in an inching stream of cars, she focused on the brighter flick of red brake lights—go and stop, go and stop.

She called home.

"Hello," Madeline answered.

"Hi. Hey, I'll be home in about 30 minutes. I'm stuck in the rush hour slog."

"Okay mom. Grandma and I are making

dinner, her spaghetti recipe, and it should be ready when you get home," Madeline said cheerfully.

"Wonderful. See you soon."

Claire clicked the call off. Madeline was changing, growing; she seemed happier, more relaxed. She laughed. She didn't hide out in her room. She brought friends to the house, good kids like Katie and Chelsea. Even more impressive, she had not complained at all, not once, about her punishment of watching her grandmother, even if it meant she could not be in the play. In fact, the two of them made the most of the punishment by taking over the grocery shopping and cooking duties, and Claire had to admit it was a major help to have them shopping and cooking. But most impressive was that her daughter had been bumped up to the TAG math class for talented and gifted students, and she was doing well in the class.

"My daughter is in the talented and gifted math class," Claire spoke into the car. "My daughter, the talented and gifted mathematician," she spoke in a matter of fact tone. No, this phrasing sounded too pretentious. The first statement with no inflection, just a slight smile, worked well. "My daughter is in the talented and gifted…." The brake lights in front of her flashed bright red. Claire, distracted, did not respond instantly, and a second later slammed her foot on the brake while simultaneously looking in the rear view mirror to ensure the white lights behind her stopped too.

"Damn it! Learn to drive!" she yelled, knowing it was her fault but feeling better by releasing her frustration. "You're tailgating! Give me space!" It felt good to yell.

Dr. Hancock had been helping tremendously. Although Madeline had asked to quit seeing him after a few sessions, Claire still saw him once a week on Mondays at 11:30 a.m. It was her secret, between her, Dr. Hancock, and her health insurance. She hadn't told John yet. She would, but not yet. This was her private time. Totally and selfishly, it was completely her time. She couldn't remember the last time, if ever, she had her own time to focus on herself.

She loved seeing Dr. Hancock. Secretly she wished she could see him two times a week. She loved how he listened intently, how he asked probing questions, how he seemed genuinely concerned. No one listened to her like he did.

She loved how his long, sleek runner's build jutted out over the angles of his chair. She loved his soft and gentle smile, his kind and wise questions. She marveled at how he seemed to hear what she could not say and know what she could not see. She wished her husband could probe and ask and care with a focused interest like Dr. Hancock.

An assigned "homework" item from Dr. Hancock involved sharing her feelings more with John and connecting more with him using non-judgmental tones and phrasing. She practiced during the evening phone call with John. "When you are not here for me, I feel sad….When you are not contributing to our income, I understand, but this makes me feel like I am carrying the full load and sometimes I feel resentful…."

Dr. Hancock also helped her feel better about Madeline. It was Dr. Hancock who helped her understand that Madeline might have needs different from her own.

Claire thought about this week's session. He had asked her to share what was most important to her without censoring her thoughts. She shared what came to mind: "Having John home, having John employed again, getting Madeline through school, doing work well, sleep, paying all the bills on time, sleep, working toward some financial security, being able to retire, maintaining her health, paying for Madeline's college education, and finding a nursing care facility for her mother." Yes, she had pushed this need to the back of her mind and her list, but her mother needed a care facility. She was near legally blind.

For several minutes, they reviewed the list, and then he asked a question that seemed unrelated to anything on the list, "How do you show Madeline that she is important to you?"

Claire wanted to respond with, "What about my list?" but she knew better. "Okay, well, I put a roof over her head," she said. She thought for a minute and then continued without pause. "I pay for her food. I pay for her clothes. I take her to the doctor. I go to teacher conferences. I earn our salary that keeps her in the middle class."

Dr. Hancock nodded as if he wanted to hear more. "I love her," she said, wondering what he wanted to hear. She kept thinking and trying to add quickly without appearing as if she were running out of ideas. "She is in the talented and gifted math class. I support this. I am trying to save for her college education. I take her on a vacation each year."

He kept nodding.

"What do you want?" she said, frustrated and immediately ashamed that it showed in her tone.

"Claire, what do you think she wants from you?

"She needs what I listed."

"Okay, help me here. What do you think is important to her?"

"I'd say a roof over her head, food on the table, clothes on her back, medical care."

"What else?"

"I love her. She knows this."

Dr. Hancock said nothing.

Claire slammed on the brakes again. Again, she had forgotten she was driving, and only remembered when she saw the bright red of a stopped car a foot from her bumper. "Damn it!" she yelled, her knees felt weak from nearly hitting a Volvo. She sat. No cars moved. She hated waiting.

Dr. Hancock had sat in silence until Claire asked again, "What!"

"What do you think?"

"I love her! What do you want?"

"What do you think she needs?" he said calmly. "I want you to think about this during the week. Can you do this for me as part of your homework? We've talked a lot about what you really want and need. This is great work. We have talked about what John wants and needs, and how you and John can work together to meet these needs. Now, what do you think is important for Madeline and for your relationship with her?"

So, here stuck in a traffic, forced to wait, bored into reflection, she thought about her homework. What else did Madeline need?

Confined in the car and unable to move, she thought and began to feel tired, very tired. She turned off the heat, needing the cold air to stay awake. A steel, cold sadness enveloped her and felt heavy on her chest. Of course, she loved Madeline, but she really didn't understand the child. She was so different than she at that age.

"What does Madeline need?"

The horn behind her honked. Claire glanced in the rearview mirror and then in front of her. The Volvo had moved a car length ahead. "Take it easy!" She yelled and pulled forward.

Then, a thought flashed into her mind. Yes, she knew what she could give her daughter. She knew! And it was a brilliant idea! And, it solved other problems on her list.

Yes, she banged the steering wheel in excitement. Madeline had handled her punishment of taking care of her grandmother with great responsibility. Every day after school she came home and spent her afternoons with her without complaint. Actually, she never complained about this, never once, which seemed remarkable. Now that Claire thought about it, this must be very hard on Madeline, taking care of an elderly person when she probably wanted to spend more time with kids her age. She had shown responsibility. She had not complained about not being in the school play. Yes, she had shown responsibility. She had served her punishment. She did her job.

Dr. Hancock was right. She needed to recognize and reward this behavior. She was a good kid. It was not natural for her to be spending all her afternoons with an old lady. She needed to hang out with other kids her own age. This wasn't right. Claire saw this clearly now.

The traffic jam broke and Claire drove along at a steady 30 miles per hour and then up to 40. She drove down the next highway exit ramp. She would be home in 10 minutes. Dr. Hancock had told her, "there are blessings in wasted time," and he had been so right. She couldn't wait to share with him that the traffic jam had given her time to think and to see what Madeline needed.

Claire decided at that moment that she would stop the punishment and reward Madeline. She knew just what to do. She would move her mother into a skilled nursing home facility, a retirement home.

Claire didn't want to do it. She loved her mother, but her mother did not have the eyesight to take care of herself, and Claire couldn't take care of her, and Madeline had served her punishment. Before the punishment and before her mother had arrived, Claire had visited all the reputable facilities in the area and had identified the top three that her mother could afford with her teacher's pension and social security. Originally, she planned to move her mother into a home soon after she arrived at their home, but the effort and guilt had been too monumental, so she put the chore on her "to do" list and ignored it because it was not a problem, until it was so far down the list that she had to scroll to see it.

But, Dr. Hancock was right, as usual. What did Madeline want? Clearly she did not want to be strapped with the burden of her grandmother. The kid had done enough and even without complaint, and kids should be having fun with their friends and not caregiving for their grandparents.

Claire felt a sadness and guilt about moving her mother into a facility, but this disappeared when an absolutely splendid idea popped into her head.

She laughed, slammed her palm on the steering wheel, and spoke the plan aloud, seeing if it sounded as good as it seemed. "This week I will take a day off work and move Mom into a retirement home. Mom and I will keep it a secret. I know just the right one—Evergreen Peaks. Yes, and I will surprise Madeline with this gift!"

Two problems solved. Dr. Hancock will be proud.

Chapter 17
Madeline's Gift

Madeline loved her new math class. Mr. Beck applied each concept they learned to something in the real world. Sometimes they worked as teams at the board to solve real-world problems; other times they studied about famous mathematicians. They learned about women mathematicians long before Grandma's time who faced extreme hardships and about careers that required math skills. Every morning she looked forward to math class—to the energy, the excitement, and the discovery. Strangely, sometimes after class, she would pass her old math classroom just as her previous teacher entered the hall. The first few times this happened she met his eyes and smiled, thinking he might be happy for her, but he didn't smile back; he looked through her as if he did not recognize her. She thought he might not. Now, she looked down and walked by him.

Now, in Mrs. Colby's class, she worked on the final exam before Christmas break. As she finished the last question, she heard the teacher's cell phone vibrate. For security and communication with the front office, each teacher carried a work-issued cell phone. "Okay, I'll tell her," Mrs. Colby said.

Madeline took her test to Mrs. Colby. "Madeline," she said softly, "That was the office. Your mother is picking you up from school right now."

Madeline immediately thought about her grandmother's health, and Mrs. Colby added quickly, "The office said not to worry, it's not an emergency at all. In fact, you can leave now. Have a wonderful Christmas break."

Grabbing her backpack from her locker, she walked to the principal's office and did not see her mother in the waiting area. One of the secretaries pointed out the main doors. Madeline understood. She walked through the doors into a clear, bright, and cold winter day and saw her mother's car, parked in the loading zone. She placed her backpack in the backseat and stepped into the car.

"Hi mom. Why are you here? Is everything okay?"

"I have a surprise for you. Put on your seatbelt."

Madeline put on her seatbelt while her mother drove away from the curb.

"A surprise?" She couldn't remember a time that her mother had left work early to meet her for anything other than necessary appointments.

"What kind of surprise?" Madeline asked, studying her mother's face for a clue.

"Honey, I have been so proud of you."

Madeline basked in the words. More than anything she wanted her mother's love, her mother's approval.

"First, I am proud of you for stepping up and displaying real responsibility in watching your grandmother. I know this wasn't easy."

"I don't mind," Madeline said, wondering what her surprise could be.

"Yes, that's another thing I am proud about. You displayed such a great attitude about watching your grandmother. You never complained."

"Mom," Madeline felt uncomfortable. She wanted the praise desperately, but she didn't "display" any attitude with Grandma. She simply enjoyed being with her.

"No, listen. You have served your punishment. You have proved to me that you can be responsible. And!" Claire said excitedly, "You worked extra hard in school and got bumped up to the gifted math class. The gifted math class! Do you know how this will help you get into college!"

Madeline hadn't thought about math class in terms of preparing her for college. She simply loved the class; however, if her mother found other benefits, she felt happy about this. She enjoyed seeing her mother relaxed and happy, which was rare.

The car pulled into the parking lot of a local nursing home. Madeline had never been into the facility before, but she recognized the ubiquitous one-story, oversized, ranch-style warehouse as an institution for the elderly.

"Okay, we're here," Claire announced as she parked the car and turned to her daughter.

Madeline glared at the nursing home, glared at her mother, and glared back at the building, suddenly terrified by what her mother had done.

It registered in a flash, and she waited silently, unable to form words, unable to process her feelings, unable to move, crushed, completely overwhelmed with dread, hoping it was not true.

"Madeline, it's not normal for a girl your age to take care of her grandmother. I realize this, and I have been working to be more receptive to your needs. I'm so proud of you," she said.

Madeline heard the words, but she couldn't think. She wanted to throw up. She wanted to run. She wanted to cry. She wanted to scream. She couldn't move. She felt blood rushing out of her head and her eyes filling with tears. She blinked.

"What's wrong?" her mother asked defensively. "Honey, what is wrong?"

Madeline could hear that her mother had no idea what was wrong. She didn't know what to do. How could she explain? "Breathe," she told herself, "breathe, and calm down." She concentrated on breathing and focused on what to do.

Her mother was talking faster now. "Honey, your grandmother cannot take care of herself. I always planned to move her into this home sometime this year, but I moved the day up to today to reward you for your good behavior. It is not normal for you to take care of her. You have your own life…"

Madeline felt sick. Her mother was still talking, but she could no longer hear her. Madeline opened the car door. The cold air felt good against her hot and sweaty skin. She stood up and stumbled away from the car. She felt dizzy and sat on the curb with her head between her knees. She gathered strength from the cold air. "Breathe," she told herself, "just breathe and don't throw up." Soon she felt her mother touching her shoulder.

"Are you alright?"

"Mom," Madeline heard her voice, but it sounded distant, "Grandma cannot drive; that's her only handicap. She can take care of herself in every other way. She can take care of herself." Even as Madeline said the words, she knew they would sting her mother.

"Young lady," Claire spoke firmly. "I love my mother. It hurts me to do this more than you will ever know, but I can't take care of her, keep a full time job, pay for your father's education, and take care of you. I can't do it all. Now, this is what is best for all of us. I thought you would be happy!"

"Mom." Madeline looked at the asphalt between her feet. It blurred as tears fell and pooled on the ground. "No one needs to take care of Grandma." She worked consciously to breathe between the words. "She can't see well, but she does everything else well. She doesn't need this yet. She is fine with us at home."

"I thought you would be happy." The words echoed in the cold air. Claire sat next to her daughter and took in a deep breath and let out a deep sigh. They both sat in silence. Madeline focused on breathing. The cold air prickled her wet skin and she shivered deeply. She felt cold from the deepest places of her being.

"Maddie, what do you want?" her mother asked, sighing. "What do you want?"

A hint of light from the afternoon sky made it through her curled-up knees and bowed head and glistened on the small lake of pooled tears at her feet. She watched color reflect in her tears, and spoke aloud but to herself, "I have been trying to find my prayer for months now."

"Still trying to find your prayer?"

"Yes. Grandma prays, and I've been watching her and trying to find my own prayer." Madeline looked up and out over the parking lot.

"I don't know much about prayer, but I think you are not limited to one. Just pick a prayer and say it." Claire said, sounding slightly annoyed.

"Mom, I want you to love me."

"I do love you."

Madeline said nothing for a moment, and Claire added, "I may not be good at showing it, but you should never question my love. I struggle, Maddie, but it is not about you. I just struggle."

"I want world peace." Madeline spoke without emotion, like some list she had been checking and double-checking for weeks.

"We all want world peace."

"I want an end to cancer and horrible disease."

"Well," Claire responded, "that's a tall order too. I guess you could become a doctor and work on that one."

"I want the end of world hunger and homelessness."

"That's another tall order," her mother said adding, "but you can get a degree in something like global studies."

Madeline thought about how her mother turned every conversation into a path to college. She paused. They sat in cold silence. "Mom, I want you to be happy."

"Well, you have no control over other people's emotions, honey," her mother replied. "That is one of those lessons we learn too late in life. I'm still learning it. I'm cold out here. Aren't you? Let's go visit Grandma, okay?"

"I want Dad to be home always, not just at Christmas break."

"He will be soon."

"I want so many things."

"We all do. We all do. In fact, I'd like a spring day." Her mother forced a laugh. "I'm freezing out here, Maddie."

"But, Mom, I have one prayer, just one prayer," and as Madeline spoke the words, she could feel the animal spirit inside her, the one that her grandmother had shown her. She could feel it for the first time. It was sheltered in her soul. She could feel it not as a deep anger but as a force, a tremendous force that bubbled up and pushed through deep sorrow and fear. It was stronger than fear. It knew her prayer. It knew what needed to be done at this moment, for this moment, and for her family for generations. She knew her prayer.

"Mama, I have one prayer," she said with a voice, her own voice, deep, strong, and sacred. She could hear her voice clearly.

Her mother said nothing. Madeline looked at her mother and wiped her tear-soaked eyes with her palms. Her mother looked scared, like she didn't know the person sitting next to her but could feel her force.

"Dear God, I have one prayer."

Madeline whispered these words with a roar.

"Dear God, help us bring my grandmother home. Amen."

And she felt her voice stretch—reverberating through generations from the voices in grandmother's stories—and pass through this exact moment and stretch out and disappear into the future. She felt the connection—*wide and long and high and deep,* and she knew *its power in her inner being*.

Chapter 18
Home

Rosemarie stood in her daughter's kitchen and listened to her granddaughter explaining to her mother how to prepare the salmon for dinner. What a crazy, unexplainable day. In the morning, moments after Madeline left for school, Claire had announced that she was moving her that morning into a "retirement center." As if describing a planned trip to Paris, she extolled the virtues of the Evergreen Peaks Assisted-Living Facility.

"Oh Mom," she said in feigned enthusiasm like bad singing, "You won't have to cook, clean, do yard work, or even laundry! It sounds like," and she paused trying to find the word, "like heaven. All your needs will be taken care of."

To Rosemarie this sounded more like hell, but there were no arguments to make. A decision had been made, and she simply sat on the edge of the bed in the guest room and watched her daughter pack her belongings and talk incessantly about the benefits of assisted living.

The entire morning was surreal and terrifying, like a tornado suddenly tearing up her life and dropping it in a retirement Oz, where smiling receptionists and young aides greeted them, bright nature photographs lined the long carpeted halls, and her room was the 10th door on the right, all decorated she thought like individual gravesites, with displays of flowers, stuffed animals, military metals, gargoyles from former travel, or some combination of past lives.

Then, as suddenly as the morning tornado had arrived, her daughter returned with Madeline in tow, greeting her nonchalantly in the same chair she landed in, and announced that she was now moving back home to live with the family. And, as only Claire could do, she said this all as if nothing unusual had happened, nothing at all.

Rosemarie could guess what might have happened, but neither of them were giving any clues. Claire seemed unusually calm, not mad as if she had lost some struggle, and not resigned, as if she had given up on some struggle. She just acted as if the morning had not happened, as if it had all been an easily fixable mistake or not a mistake at all, just part of a normal and routine day.

And Madeline, well, she seemed different. Her voice sounded more full and confident and relaxed, as if nothing out of the ordinary had happened that day, or any day before, as if it were all going to be okay.

As she watched the women she loved, Rosemarie caught glimpses of her grand-daughter's light, flashes of kaleidoscope color dancing around within the meal preparation movements. She could see that something had changed, something indistinguishable to the world, but real and significant in Rosemarie's sight. She simply stood aside and watched, relaxing for the first time in a very long while.

Claire could not believe her daughter's question: "Is it Atlantic or Pacific salmon?" What kind of kid cares what kind of salmon it is?

"Salmon is salmon," Claire replied. "It all tastes the same."

"I am sure the fish cares," said Madeline,

adding the next instruction. "Cut here on the fin, Mom. Not too high."

Claire stood at the cutting board next to her daughter, following each instruction, one clearly articulated step at a time, and in the cutting, bumped against her daughter's shoulder. In this clumsy exchange, in an act of love, each leaned into the other, shoulder to shoulder, holding the other's balance for a moment. Claire rested the knife on the cutting board, both hands spread along the sides of the board.

"You okay, Mom?"

Claire nodded, overcome with emotion for her daughter. For reasons unknown and that she regretted even in that moment, she hid her pride, picked up the knife, and cut. She cut slowly and purposefully, totally aware that it had been a long time, too long a time, since she had felt in a moment, even a fleeting moment, relaxed and happy. Sadly, she felt the moment would pass too quickly, but it was a moment, and there would be others, and it was enough, This had been a very, very good day.

Madeline watched her mother carefully and deliberately follow each instruction, not rushed, just involved in the task. She could feel her grandmother watching her and smiled back, but Grandma missed the cue and simply stared at her, seemingly relaxed and knowing. It would have been spooky from anyone else, but her unseeing gaze felt warming, like a light.

Madeline stood in the moment with nothing to do but watch. Rain pelted the roof. Taking in a deep breath and feeling the moment, she knew that this was the end of an adventure that would someday be a story she could tell. She felt the story rest within her.

She knew that tomorrow, and probably even later tonight, her mother would get worked up about some financial issue or some work project that had fallen behind schedule. She knew that her grandmother had heart problems. She knew some new problem awaited her just around the corner. However, at this one moment, she felt home, completely home, and she knew, like the stories of her relatives before her, they would all be okay.

35571005R00134

Made in the USA
Lexington, KY
16 September 2014